PAINTED LADIES

A Chase Adams FBI Thriller

Book 7

Patrick Logan

Books by Patrick Logan

Detective Damien Drake

Book 1: Butterfly Kisses

Book 2: Cause of Death

Book 3: Download Murder

Book 4: Skeleton King

Book 5: Human Traffic

Book 6: Drug Lord: Part One

Book 7: Drug Lord: Part Two

Book 8: Prized Fight

Book 9: Almost Infamous

Dr. Beckett Campbell, ME

Book 0: Bitter End

Book 1: Organ Donor

Book 2: Injecting Faith

Book 3: Surgical Precision

Book 4: Do Not Resuscitate

Book 5: Extracting Evil

First Edition: September 2019

Prologue

"LOOK AT THIS FAGGOT right here," the man in the overcoat said with a chuckle. "Hey fellas, come take a look at this guy."

He extended his finger at a man sporting skinny jeans and a white T-shirt. His hair was slicked back, and his chin was pressed to his chest in a deliberate attempt to avoid eye contact with the three approaching thugs.

"Where you comin' from, homo?" One of the other men demanded. "Bet you it's one of those faggot bars over on thirty-first."

Despite the cool fall air, only the first man was wearing a coat. The others donned ratty sweatshirts or, in the case of the man with the slicked hair, just a T-shirt.

"Hey, Ronnie asked you a question, faggot," the first man said.

The third member of the trio, a gangly fellow with wide eyes and a patchy mustache, finally joined into the fray.

"Hey, you got a fuckin' problem with your ears or somethin'?"

Ronnie reached for the man in the white T-shirt, but his hand was immediately swatted away.

"I don't want any trouble. I just wanna get home."

"You hit me," Ronnie said, incredulous. "This fucker hit me. You seen that, Mike? Mike, you seen that?"

"I don't want any trouble," the man repeated, holding his hands up defensively. "Just wanna get home."

Mike growled and tucked the tails of his overcoat behind his back.

"Why the fuck did you hit him? He didn't do nothin' to you."

"He was trying to grab me. Like I said, I just want to go home."

With that, he tried to step around the three men, but Mike deliberately blocked his path.

"Please, just let me by."

"I want you to apologize first; I want you to apologize to Ronnie."

The man in the T-shirt lifted his eyes and stared at Mike. Then he looked at the other two men. The latter were soft, wannabes.

Followers.

But Mike… he had an icy stare that meant business.

"Sorry—didn't mean nothing by it," he said at last, trying to diffuse the situation.

He tried to slip by again, but Mike held out his hand and placed it in the center of his chest, halting his progress.

The man knew better than to slap his hand away, as he had done with Ronnie moments ago.

"That's good," Mike said, a sneer appearing on his face. "That's real good. Now get on your knees."

"W-w-what?"

"I said, get on your fucking knees, faggot."

The two followers chuckled and the man in the T-shirt shook his head.

"Man—look, you guys have been drinking, I—I mean, I just want to go home." He was trying not to sound desperate, but the situation was about to escalate. Looking around, he was dismayed to see that the few shops nearby had all closed down for the night. "Please, I—"

Mike wasn't just big, but he was fast, too. His hand shot out and he grabbed a fistful of the man's hair. Then he shoved him to his knees while pulling back at the same time, stretching his throat until it started to ache.

"Yeah, that's a good boy," Mike breathed. To the man's horror, he started to unzip the front of his jeans with his free hand.

"Please," the man croaked, his eyes starting to water. "Please, let me go."

"I'll let you go when I'm done with you."

With that, Mike pulled his flaccid penis out and dangled it in front of his face. He tried to look away, but his face was forced forward by the hand tangled in his hair.

"You like what you see?" Mike asked.

"Yeah, he likes it, he likes it," Ronnie said almost giddily.

"Yeah, I know he does," Mike confirmed, pulling the man's face even closer. He tried to turn away, but the grip on his hair was so tight that—

All of a sudden, his head was wrenched backward, and his legs folded beneath him awkwardly as he fell onto his back.

"I told you he was a faggot," Mike said.

The man in the white T-shirt struggled to collect himself and get back to his feet when a massive fist came out of nowhere and struck him directly between the eyes.

"Yeah, I told you," was the last thing he heard before falling back to the pavement, unconscious.

***

"I think we're gonna hit the rippers for a bit. You wanna join, Mikey?" Ronnie asked.

Mike shook his head.

"Can't—gotta work in the morning." He checked his watch and then chuckled dryly. "In a few hours." As he spoke, he massaged his right hand. The middle knuckle was sore, and he wondered briefly if he had broken it by punching the fag in the face. This made him nervous; if it swelled up, he might be unable to grip the pitchfork properly. And if that were the case, his dad would be fucking incensed.

"I gotta get going," he said quickly.

"Alright, catch you later," Ronnie replied as he turned back the way they'd come. "Nice punch, by the way."

Mike slipped his hands into his overcoat pockets, then he picked up the pace.

After about ten minutes of brisk walking, the storefronts were all but gone. Five minutes after that, Mike found himself squeezing through an opening in a chain-link fence. He was familiar with the cornfield before him: it belonged to a curmudgeonly farmer named Laurence Finnegan. Mike didn't know him well, but his dad often had a beer with the man during the summer months. They even shared old farm equipment on occasion. All this to say, that Mike was confident that he was unlikely to receive a chest full of buckshot by cutting through the man's field.

Or so he hoped.

"Old faggot," he grumbled.

The field was only about fifty yards across, but the height and breadth of the corn stalks made walking difficult. Just as Mike was second-guessing his decision to take the shortcut, he heard a rustling to his left.

He fell still and craned his neck in direction of the sound. His first thought was that it was just a fox, but when he didn't see anything, Mike's heart began to beat a little faster.

He read a story once that there had been coyote sightings in every major city in the United States.

And that included New York City.

Swallowing hard, Mike started to walk again, this time shoving stalks out of the way to speed his progress. He'd taken only a handful of steps before stopping once more.

The sound was back, and this time it didn't sound like either a fox or a coyote.

This time it sounded like something larger.

"Who's there?" He demanded, trying to sound authoritative. Worried that the words had come out weak, he cleared his throat and repeated the question. "Who's there?"

For the better part of a minute, Mike stood as still as possible and listened. The only sound he heard was the gentle rustling of the corn stalks and his own breathing.

Get a fucking grip, you pussy.

Mike took a single step before the stalks to his right suddenly parted and a figure burst through. He had just enough time to brace himself for impact, but the man didn't collide with him as he expected.

Instead, he passed by and disappeared into the corn on the other side.

"The fuck?"

Mike watched the spot where the man had disappeared until the stalks stopped swaying. Only then did he look down at himself.

If it hadn't been for the gash in his trench coat, he might have passed the entire thing off as a sort of drunken mirage. But when he put a hand to the slit and then held his fingers up to the light, he knew that what had happened was very real.

Blood coated the pads of his fingers.

"What the fuck!"

His heart racing now, Mike whipped his head around, desperate to spot his assailant.

"Is that you, you fucking faggot? Come out here and fight me like a man!" he yelled. The threat had meant to bolster his resolve, but the tremulous sound of his voice only made him more frightened. "Come out and—"

The figure emerged from directly in front of him, but once again, he was too quick and slipped by before Mike could grab a hold of him. It didn't help that the man was slippery like he was covered in some sort of Vaseline—there was simply nothing to grab on to.

Mike realized that he'd been cut again, across his chest this time, and covered the wound with his forearm.

"What the—"

The figure came from behind, crouching now, and sliced Mike's left hamstring clean through. He cried out in pain and dropped to his knees. Forgetting all about his other wounds, he clutched the back of his leg with both hands.

"Please," he said desperately. "I don't mean what I—"

The corn parted directly in front of him and a man stepped into full view of the moonlight. And that's when Mike realized his error; he wasn't covered in Vaseline but sweat. And he wasn't the same man whom Mike had punched in the face earlier.

In fact, Mike had never seen him before in his life.

He was completely nude and impossibly pale. The only color on the man at all was a small tuft of brown hair in the center of his concave chest and equally dark pubic hair. His penis hung limply between his legs, but he had no testicles to speak of.

"What the hell?" Mike gasped.

In each one of the man's hands was a long, pointed knife.

"What—w-w-what do you want?" Mike asked. He tried to stand, but his injured leg refused to support him, and he fell back to his knees. "Who the fuck are you?"

The only answer came in the form of a high-pitched laugh.

PART I – The First Kill

Chapter 1

"YOU CAN TAKE WHOEVER you want, Chase. Seriously, whoever and whatever you need is yours."

FBI Special Agent Chase Adams stared into Director Hampton's eyes. She'd burst through the door and shown him the photograph of Louisa and Stitts, as well as the accompanying text—*Chase, I've missed you*—and the man hadn't batted an eye.

He didn't ask who the text was from, why they'd sent it to her, or even when she'd received it.

Director Hampton had simply given her carte blanche to use all of the FBI resources. The only problem was, the person that Chase wanted wasn't in the Bureau.

"Whoever I want?" she asked.

One of Director Hampton's eyebrows rose a little—it was nothing more than a glorified twitch, really—but he concurred with a nod.

The man was cold and calculated, and if the rumors about him were true, at one time, he had been the best Agent in the entire Bureau.

His loyalty had never been in doubt. His unconventional methods with the recruits, on the other hand…

"Whoever you want," Director Hampton repeated. "I know you're close with Floyd, so you can take him with you. You want someone else? Just tell me their names and I'll pull them off whatever case they're on and give them to you."

Chase stared at the man a little longer. Then she shook her head.

She couldn't get Floyd involved in this. He was just a kid, and she felt responsible for him. Floyd had nearly died back in Washington, and while he had been helpful in New Mexico, the last Agent that she'd worked with—Stacy Workman—had ended up dead.

And that said nothing of Stitts, who was bound and gagged and being held God knows where.

Her conscience couldn't handle another death.

"No, not Floyd—someone else. I think," Chase hesitated, once again meeting the Director's hard stare, "I think you're going to have to make some calls on this one."

Chase half-expected the man to ask for more details, to question her, to ask her to explain her reasoning. But Director Hampton surprised her by immediately picking up the phone on his desk.

"Who am I calling?"

"Not who, but where," Chase said, pressing her lips together tightly. "You need to call New York City—62nd precinct, to be exact. I'm going back."

Chapter 2

"Rise and shine, cupcake," the officer said as he banged his nightstick against the iron bars.

The man in the cell looked up and then grunted as he pulled himself to a seated position.

"Where we going?"

The officer chuckled.

"For a little ride—we're going for a little ride."

The prisoner stretched his back and his arms, then rose to his feet. He started toward the cell door but stopped when the officer pointed the business end of a nightstick toward his chest.

"Turn around, hands through the bars," the officer instructed. The prisoner grimaced but did as he was told, sliding his wrists through the slot that they slid a tray of food through twice a day. The cuffs were slapped on his wrists, one click too tight.

"Alright, get the fuck out here."

The prisoner stepped away from the bars and then waited for the door to be unlocked. Once in the hallway, the officer spun him around and shoved him forward. His legs were still half-asleep, and he nearly pitched onto his face.

"Keep moving."

He bit back a scathing remark.

If I didn't have these cuffs on…

As he made his way through the familiar hallways of 62nd precinct, the prisoner kept his eyes low. He knew that others were staring at him, trying to get his attention, but he refused to take the bait.

After all, they weren't his colleagues anymore, or his friends. They were his captors, the ones who held the keys to his freedom.

And they weren't about to let him go.

Not just yet, anyway.

The prisoner was shoved through the front doors and immediately squinted and turned his face away from the bright sunlight. His cell was near the heart of the police station and the only illumination that he'd been exposed to for the past two days had been from a weak incandescent bulb.

This was torture. For a fall day, New York City had never been so bright, it seemed.

Still, he enjoyed the fresh air and sucked in deep breaths until the moment he was thrust into the back of an awaiting vehicle.

The officer who had pulled him from his cell slammed the door closed, a grimace on his fat face.

"Where are you taking me?" he demanded as the car pulled out of the parking lot. "You taking me to my arraignment?"

There was no answer, but something wasn't right about this scenario. Usually, suspects weren't driven to the courthouse in the back of an unmarked car. Even with his checkered past and notoriety, this was unconventional, at best.

At worst, it was a hit.

"Hey? Where are you taking me?" he repeated as he sat up and tried to get comfortable. With his hands nearly numb and pressed up against the cracked vinyl seat, it was a fool's errand.

He was about to ask again when his gaze drifted to the heavily tinted windows.

New York City, he thought glumly. *You are as much a piece of me as my cirrhotic liver.*

The prisoner was familiar with the route to the courthouse from a different time, a different era, even, and he knew that this wasn't it.

The car swerved and sped down a filthy alleyway, barely avoiding an overflowing dumpster.

"Listen, you fu—"

Before he could finish the sentence, a dark BMW appeared out of nowhere, forcing the unmarked police car to squeal to a stop. Instead of honking the horn or shouting obscenities out the window, the driver calmly threw an arm over the headrest and turned.

"Detective Dunbar?"

The man smiled and nodded.

"It's been a while," Detective Stephen Dunbar said, still grinning. "Way too fucking long."

Thinking that he was perhaps hallucinating, the prisoner shook his head and blinked rapidly. Detective Dunbar's smiling face didn't waver.

"There's someone else that wants to say hi."

With that, the detective turned and pointed out the windshield at the BMW.

He followed the man's gaze and watched as the driver's side door opened and a woman got out.

His jaw fell slack.

She was short, with shoulder-length brown hair and bright green eyes.

"Chase?"

Chapter 3

SHE ALMOST DIDN'T RECOGNIZE him. The man who had been her partner in the NYPD, the person responsible for spring boarding her career into the FBI, was but a shell of the person Chase Adams had grown to know and love and depend on.

Damien Drake had a short beard that accentuated his square jaw and hollow eyes. He was also thinner than she remembered but, to her surprise, he actually looked healthier. Ironic, given the diet they must have fed him in prison.

She watched as Detective Dunbar helped him from the car and then removed his cuffs. Her ex-partner even seemed to move differently. Back in their NYPD days, he was always in a hurry, as if he took one second longer than he had to, bad things would happen.

And sometimes they did.

Now, however, every one of his steps seemed deliberate, purposeful. As if these simple movements were a gift like he was on borrowed time.

Something happened to him. Something changed him.

"Drake," Chase said, trying not to sound desperate.

The man looked at her, confusion masking his handsome face, and then he stepped forward.

Chase mimicked his movements, keeping her hands, which were covered in black leather gloves, pushed deep into her pockets.

"Chase? Chase, what's going on here?"

"I missed—" *you, too,* she was about to say, before Drake surprised her by wrapping his big arms around her and squeezing tightly.

Chase nearly fell backward, but his grip was strong. When the embrace stretched on for the better part of a minute, she pulled her hands out of her pockets and hugged him back. Over Drake's shoulder, she caught Dunbar looking at them, eyebrows raised. As if sensing this, Drake gave her a final squeeze and finally let go.

"Jesus, how long has it been?"

Chase looked away, embarrassed.

As with Stitts, she'd been so engrossed in her own problems that she hadn't even once reached out to the man and asked about his.

Chase knew a little of what he'd been through—Dunbar had given her the lowdown—but there was so much that she didn't know, that she *should've* known, given how close they'd once been.

"Too long," she said at last.

"Yeah, way too long."

The two of them just stood in the alley for several moments, hands dangling at their sides before Drake broke the silence.

"You gonna tell me what's going on here?" he asked. "Because I have no—"

"I need your help," Chase said suddenly, her eyes returning to Drake's. "Drake, I really need your help."

Drake's jaw flexed and he nodded.

"Yeah, I thought you might say that. I know a good place not too far from here where we can go and chat." He hooked a chin over his shoulder at Dunbar. "Away from prying eyes and listening ears, of course."

Chapter 4

"JUST A COFFEE, BLACK," Chase said as the elderly waitress approached. The woman with thin gray hair was gnawing on a piece of gum like a hunk of cud. She acknowledged the request with a simple nod, then turned to Drake.

"And for you? The usual?"

The usual?

Drake shook his head.

"Just a coffee. Also black."

The waitress cracked her gum then hurried off. When they were alone once more, Chase withdrew a folder and laid out a series of images on the table. They were all blown up sections of the same original photograph.

She watched intently as Drake leaned forward, squinting, then held up one of the photos up to his face.

"Jeremy Stitts," he said simply.

Chase nodded.

"Yeah, someone got him, Drake." Chase tapped the female in another image. "This is my friend Louisa—they got them both." Her voice hitched. "The photo was sent from Louisa's phone two days ago. The phone has since been shut off and the SIM card removed. I doubt it'll come back online again."

"Where was it sent from?" Drake asked, all business now.

"Somewhere in New York City. Whoever is responsible must have grabbed Louisa and Stitts and brought them here, somehow. Just our luck, something fucked up with the cell tower pings and the techs have been unable to narrow it down more than that. Just 'NYC'. Big fucking place, this New York City."

Drake frowned.

"Why bring them all the way to New York? Seems like a huge risk."

Chase shrugged.

"No fucking clue."

After Drake paused to let this sink in, he said, "Was there a message to go along with the photo?"

Chase pulled out another sheet of paper and handed it over.

"Chase, I've missed you," Drake whispered.

The words were haunting, even coming from him.

"We've got nothing, Drake. No clues, no suspects. All we know is that it's personal."

Drake leaned back a little, but his eyes remained locked on hers.

Chase knew that Drake and Stitts didn't really get along, but she also knew that Drake was one of the most loyal people on this earth.

He would help her.

He *had* to.

"And so, you came to me," he said.

Chase nodded.

"My boss has given me free rein on this... but because it's personal, I'm going to need people I can trust. And, unfortunately, the list of individuals who fit that bill isn't very long."

"What about my legal troubles? Surely you've heard—"

Chase waved a hand dismissively.

"Like I said, anyone I want. For now, you're a special consultant to the FBI." Chase emphasized the words, *for now*, hoping that Drake would understand. Director Hampton had literally pulled every single string he could find to get Drake released on bail, but getting his charges of assault and battery and unlawful confinement of a police officer dropped entirely?

Not even he had that sort of sway.

"Well, I've been out of the game for a while," Drake said.

The waitress returned with their coffees and set them on the table. As Drake reached for his, the gray-haired women stared at him expectantly.

"I'm fine," he said.

The waitress scowled and left them alone.

"I don't have many connections, and I have even fewer friends," Drake continued. "But I'm good at tracking people."

Chase nodded enthusiastically.

This is what she'd hoped the man would say. They hadn't seen each other for more than two years, and while Drake appeared to have changed both physically and mentally, his loyalty had never waned.

They'd been partners on several high-profile cases—the Download Killer and Craig Sloan, the medical resident turned serial killer, to name a few—and they'd been close. There had even been a time when their relationship had threatened to become something more, but at the time, she'd been happily married.

Chase shook her head. Her mind tended to wander with a lack of sleep.

"Alright, let's start at the beginning," Drake said. "But first, you want to tell me why you're wearing gloves inside?"

Chapter 5

"SO, THAT'S IT—THAT'S all I know. As soon as I got the message, I flew from Albuquerque to Virginia. From there, I went directly into the Director's office."

Chase watched as Drake soaked in everything she'd told him. She hadn't revealed all the details about what had happened in New Mexico—she'd left out the part about her being tied up and shocked as well as Stacy Workman's murder—but had told him that she and Stitts were having 'issues'.

She'd also glossed over why, exactly, she was prone to wear gloves no matter the weather.

"So, you and Stitts were fighting, huh? I'm guessing that you haven't made a whole lot of friends in the FBI, am I right?"

"What can I say, I haven't changed as much as you have."

Their friendly banter was stilted, but it had always been a staple of their relationship and Chase went with it, even though her reply wasn't actually true.

She *had* changed, and in more ways than one. Chase had kicked her heroin addiction, had buried some, if not most of her demons, and had even stopped using her body to get what she wanted.

Barring a few notable exclusions, that is.

"And you have no idea who would want to hurt you like this? Who not only had the means but the motive to kidnap your friend and partner?" Drake asked.

She shook her head.

"You can't think of a single person?"

Chase chewed her lip as she thought about this for a moment.

A single person?

There was William Woodley, disgruntled ex-secret service Tanner Pratt, FBI Agent Bellefontaine, who probably blamed her for his partner Stacy Workman's death, and then there was Brian Jalston, but at least he was locked up.

"Can I think of *one* person? No. I can think of many."

Drake made a face; they both knew that too many suspects were the same as too few—maybe even worse.

"Look, I get that you came to me because you trust me, that you don't know who is involved and don't want to tip anyone off. I get that. I'm going to find your friend and partner, Chase, that's a promise… *eventually.*" He gestured at the photograph of Stitts and Louisa. "I just don't know how much time we have. We *need* help with this. We need to get others involved, others we can trust."

Chase hated what Drake was saying but knew deep down that it was true. She had no idea what the motive behind the kidnappings was, but if it was just to hurt her then Stitts and Louisa were as good as dead already. If it was something else, there was a chance that they were still alive.

For now—they needed to act fast, and they needed help.

But she still refused to get Floyd involved. The risk was simply too great.

So, who did that leave? There was Stu Barnes, of course, her rich benefactor from Las Vegas, but she doubted he could do more than offer financial support. This might come in handy, but it wasn't enough.

Pete Horrowitz from the ATF, maybe? Terrence Conway of the TBI?

The list was short, incomplete.

Fuck. It's times like these I wish I'd made a few more friends along the way.

Chase gave up.

"You have anyone in mind?" Chase asked as she sipped her coffee. It was burnt and thick like tar, but it was also strong, which was what she needed.

"Yeah, one in particular: a weird medical examiner with tattoos. I'm sure that he'd be willing to help us out. And we can trust him... *mostly.*"

Chapter 6

New York had been Chase Adams' home for only a short while, but she was familiar with the city. She'd been to NYU Med several times, almost exclusively to interact with Dr. Beckett Campbell, head Medical Examiner for New York State.

She liked him. He was strange, he was out there, but he was dependable. And if Drake said he was trustworthy-*ish* then she took his word for it.

What's more, is that Chase had already gone to bat for the man. After Beckett had been found with a bloody rock in his hand and serial killer Craig Sloan's body at his feet, she'd helped guide him through the subsequent Internal Affairs investigation.

With her direction, Beckett hadn't even been officially reprimanded for his… suspicious… behavior.

"Haven't been here in a while," Drake remarked.

"Same. How sure are you that Beckett still works here? I mean, it's just as likely that he pissed someone important off and got his ass fired."

Chase meant the comment as a joke, but Drake didn't laugh.

"Who knows with that guy—but if he's here, we can count on him."

It sounded as if Drake was trying to convince himself, as well as Chase.

She knew that Beckett had lost most of one finger at the hands of the Church of Liberation and wouldn't be surprised if the man held Drake at least partly responsible. Their friendship went way back, but there had been some fairly large bumps in the road along the way.

This realization brought up her own feelings pertaining to Stitts.

I should've never slept with him. If I hadn't slept with him, Stitts would have stayed with me in New Mexico. And if he'd stayed…

"Well, there's only one way to find out if Beckett's still gainfully employed," Chase said as she pulled the doors open and gestured for Drake to enter.

***

"Hello? Anyone here?"

Even though they were familiar with the building, it took twenty minutes to find the pathology department.

Everything just looked so damn similar.

Once there, they'd found the secretary's desk unoccupied. Aside from a picture of a large, smiling woman clutching Chris Hemsworth around the waist, it didn't look like anybody had been there for some time.

"Hello?"

There was still no reply.

"His office is over here," Drake suggested, moving away from the desk, and starting down a narrow hallway.

Chase looked at the names listed beside the doors that they passed—Dr. Hollenbeck, Dr. Nordmeyer, Dr. Flintstein—and couldn't help but think back to the old curmudgeon that Drake had saved along with Suzan in the burning house all those years ago.

It was in the light of these flames that Beckett had bashed Craig Sloan's head in with a rock.

Drake stopped in front of the last door before the emergency stairwell and put his hands on his hips.

"Huh," he said, cocking his head to one side. "This used to be his office."

Chase's eyes drifted to the spot where the names of the other doctors had been.

It was blank.

"Shit, maybe he *was* fired."

As much as she wanted to find Beckett, they simply didn't have the time to search for him, especially given the fact that the man was as unpredictable as they came.

"Can you think of anyone else that—"

"Hold up, there's one more place we should check," Drake said as he backed away from the door.

"Yeah? Where's that?"

"The morgue," Drake said flatly.

***

The thing about being an FBI agent was that while it was far from a sexy career, people perceived it as such. And the badge featuring the iconic FBI logo? TV had done wonders for convincing people that it was pretty much a pass to anywhere you wanted to go.

Like the morgue, for instance, which was typically reserved for the ME, coroner, and lab techs.

Shit, the DA wasn't even allowed down here.

But Chase had no problems gaining access.

The elevator pinged and she stepped out, moving quickly. She hoped to see Beckett's head of spiky blond hair pop up from behind a gurney but was disappointed.

Other than a diminutive figure with their back to Chase and Drake, there was not another living soul in the morgue.

"Dr. Campbell?" she asked, even though she knew that it wasn't him.

The figure in the green smock who was hunkered over a corpse was too small to be Beckett. Worried that she might frighten the doctor, Chase cleared her throat and then stepped forward and raised her voice.

"Dr. Campbell?"

The figure turned.

"You can't be in here," the woman snapped. The giant shield in front of her face gave her words a strange sonic quality that made Chase's eardrums vibrate.

"We're looking for Dr. Campbell."

The woman crinkled her nose.

"You can't be in here," she repeated.

Chase held up her badge.

"FBI—we're looking for Dr. Campbell."

As she waited for a response, Chase leaned to her left and peered around the mousy woman. On the gurney lay a man in his late twenties. His face was covered in white makeup and his lips were painted a deep red. He looked like a cross between a clown and a transvestite.

The doctor moved to block her view.

"Is this about Bob Bumacher?"

Chase could feel her frustration mounting as the woman continued to avoid her questions. She could only imagine how Beckett managed to deal with someone like this.

"Who? I'm looking for Beckett."

"What about Bob Bumacher?" Drake suddenly asked, stepping forward. "He was killed during a break-in."

The woman's eyebrows knitted, which served to completely shroud her beady eyes.

"Who are you?" she asked.

"Who the fuck are you?" Drake shot back.

Well, that answers that question: Drake hasn't lost his subtlety or tact.

"My name's Dr. Karen Nordmeyer, head ME for New York State. Now, if you don't—"

"As I said, Dr. Nordmeyer, we're looking for—wait, *head* medical examiner?"

The woman smiled proudly.

"Yes, I'm the new—"

"What happened to Beckett?" Drake suddenly demanded. Chase tried to stop him from moving forward, but he simply stepped around her hand and hovered over the medical examiner.

"I'm sorry, but Dr. Campbell... Dr. Campbell's dead—he died a few days ago."

Chapter 7

THIS TIME WHEN DRAKE tried to move forward, Chase got directly in front of him, even though she was still reeling from what Dr. Nordmeyer had just said.

Beckett's dead?

"What the hell are you talking about?" Drake nearly shouted. Dr. Nordmeyer cowered and at this point, it looked as if Drake saw the body on the gurney for the first time.

"No," he gasped. "It can't—it's not..."

Chase put a hand on her friend's shoulder.

"It's not him, Drake."

It wasn't just the bizarre makeup that gave her the confidence to say this, but also the fact that his arms were devoid of tattoos. There was, however, some sort of crude shape drawn in what looked like blood on his chest.

"It's not Beckett."

Drake, appearing to come to the same conclusion, straightened. But before he could say anything, the ME spoke up again.

"Are you investigating him?"

Drake's brow furrowed.

"Investigate him? What the hell are you talking about? I don't know if you think this is funny, or something, but it's not. Get your head screwed on straight and tell us where Beckett is."

The woman looked around uncomfortably.

"I'm sorry, but this isn't a joke—he's dead. Dr. Campbell collapsed in this very hospital two days ago. There was nothing anyone could do."

Chase suddenly found it difficult to swallow.

He's really dead?

Somehow, she found her voice.

"Jesus, how did he die?"

Dr. Nordmeyer shrugged.

"I'm not sure."

Drake's body suddenly tensed.

"You're not sure? You're the head fucking ME, and you don't know how he died? What the fuck's going on here?"

Chase adjusted her hand on Drake's back to comfort him, but it didn't seem to make a difference.

"They took his body—I haven't seen it. I, uhh, I need to get back to work, so…"

There was no, *I'm sorry for your loss,* or *it was sad to see him go, so unexpected. So young.*

Nothing. Not a shred of empathy in this woman.

"What the fuck is your problem?" Drake barked.

Dr. Nordmeyer pursed her lips.

"I need to get back to work. FBI or not, you can't be—"

Drake leaned forward again and Dr. Nordmeyer, desperate to get out of his way, bumped into the gurney behind her. This caused it to move slightly, revealing more of the corpse lying on top.

"You're a real piece of work, you know that? You can't even—" Drake paused, and then shuffled to his right. "What the—what the hell is that?"

Chase's eyes followed his gaze and then she felt her heart palpitate in her chest.

"What the fuck?"

"Excuse me, unless you want me to call—"

No way.

"A butterfly," Chase gasped.

Now it was Drake's turn to support her.

The drawing on the corpse's chest was messy and rudimentary, but it was, undoubtedly, a butterfly: it consisted of a cylindrical-like body and two sets of wings that looked like opposing capital 'B's. There were even two long antennae that extended to the hollow of the man's throat.

Her knees suddenly felt week, and she leaned on Drake to keep from stumbling.

"Did you do this?" Drake asked as he wrapped an arm around Chase's waist. "Did you do this?"

Dr. Nordmeyer's entire face seemed to suck inward.

"What? *No*. I'm nothing like *him*—this body came in early this morning. Was just about to start to autopsy. Please, you need to leave."

Chase felt as if she was in a dream now, her body moving without any conscious input.

"You need to leave—wait, no, you can't—please, stay away from the body. No, no—keep your gloves on! No, you can't—hello? You can't touch the body! You can't do that!"

Chapter 8

"**CHASE?**"

Chase squeezed her eyes together tightly, trying to picture the victim as he... *what? Ran? Walked? Drove?* Through the... *Woods? Streets? Abandoned warehouse?* Before being approached by... a *man? Woman? Someone he knows? A stranger?*

"Chase?"

Stars speckled across her vision as she tried to block out Drake's voice.

What happened to you? Were you coming home from the bar?

Chase thought she picked up the faint odor of alcohol, but it was low down, buried beneath the reek of formalin.

Did someone offer you a ride home?

She shook her head.

No, you're a big, solidly built man. You wouldn't accept a ride by—

A hand came down on her shoulder, and Chase whipped around her.

"Chase?"

Drake was staring at her, the inner corners of his eyebrows high on his forehead. At first, she thought that this was concern on the man's face, but then she remembered that he wasn't Stitts—he didn't know about her 'voodoo'.

The 'voodoo' that she'd apparently lost.

No, this was something else.

Guilt.

"What? What is it?"

"You can't touch the body. Not without gloves," Dr. Nordmeyer interrupted. "You—"

Drake turned to the woman.

"Would you just shut the fuck up, for once?" Then, to Chase, he said, "There's something you need to know."

Chase's eyes drifted to the butterfly drawn on the corpse's chest.

She inhaled deeply.

"Yeah?"

"Yeah. But not here—somewhere more private."

Chase was about to object, to say that she needed to touch the body again, to let her subconscious take over.

But it was gone. That part of her… when Lance O'Neill had jammed the cattle prod into her chest, something must have happened to her internal circuitry.

Her brain had been rearranged.

Corrected.

Broken.

The real question was, was she better off without her special talent?

"Okay," she said softly. "Okay."

As Drake led her to the elevator, Dr. Nordmeyer hollered after them.

"I'm putting this in the report! I'm not going to lie! Not after what Beckett did! I'm reporting this!"

The sentence gave Chase pause, but Drake gently put his hand on her back and ushered her into the metal box.

Just before the elevator doors pinged closed, Drake gave the doctor a middle finger salute.

***

Barney's had found a happy medium, it seemed. It wasn't the old-timey pub that it had once been, nor was it a neon nightmare. Instead, it had modern decor, but the music was relaxing and the lighting soft.

Drake ordered a scotch, and Chase a beer. They sat sipping their drinks in silence for several moments, despite the urgency of the situation.

Chase was having a hard time wrapping her mind around the day's events. She still held out hope that Beckett was alive, that the bitch at the morgue was either high or had the most twisted sense of humor since Wayne Gacy.

And the butterfly… that was just a coincidence, wasn't it?

Chase closed her eyes and visions of her first case as a detective in New York appeared. She was tied to a pole, a filthy rag shoved in her mouth. A psychopath stood to her right, threatening to make her his final victim.

To finally complete his revenge for something that had happened to him when he was a child.

Marcus Slasinsky—Dr. Mark Kruk—whose mind had broken when his mother had died, and maggots started to eat her corpse. He was tormented by his peers, covered in butterflies…

She shook her head. This couldn't be related, because Marcus Slasinsky was locked away and would be for the rest of his natural life.

Chase looked at Drake.

"What is it? What's so important that you dragged me all the way here?"

Drake sighed. He looked better, healthier than she'd ever seen him, but there was a darkness inside the man that hadn't been there even after his partner had been murdered.

"There's something—fuck," he pinched the bridge of his nose. "It's fucked up Chase, I…"

Chase scowled.

"Drake, spit it out. I know you've been through some rough times—shit, we both have. Now this Beckett thing... but right now, my priority is finding Stitts and Louisa. Everything else... callous as it sounds, everything else can wait. I just—"

Drake leveled his eyes at her, and Chase froze. He wasn't healthier, not by a long shot.

"I've done some things in my life, Chase, things that I'm not proud of. But I've always *tried* to do the right thing, even if it meant making certain sacrifices—for me or for others. And I'll be the first to admit, not all my decisions worked out, but I—"

Chase's frustration came to a head.

"Drake, just fucking say it. No beating about the bush, whatever you've done—"

"I know who took your friends, Chase."

Chase's mouth fell open.

"You *what*? How could you—"

"I know who took your friends because I helped him escape."

Chapter 9

"**WHAT—WHAT THE HELL** are you talking about?" Chase gasped. She flailed her arms and knocked her half-full beer over. "Drake, you can't be fucking serious."

Drake moved away from the beer that ran off the table and nearly landed on his lap.

"I'm sorry—I never would have given that piece of shit anything if I thought he would ever get out."

"Get out? Wait—wait, you *helped* him get out. You helped Marcus Slasinsky, a fucking psychopath who once held a gun to my head, a man who killed four people, get out… but only after you gave him, what? Trinkets of mine? Fucking *hair*? For what? So he could beat off to me in the psych ward?"

Drake swallowed hard, confirming that what Chase had just said was a fairly accurate summarization. It still didn't make it any less fucked up, though.

"Jesus, where did you even get my stuff? My fucking *hair?*"

Drake shook his head.

"It doesn't matter, I took a calculated risk and—"

Chase was close to flying across the table and throttling her ex-partner now.

"Really? A calculated risk? Not your risk, mind you, but *my* risk. You fucking fed this man's obsession about me without my permission! That's not a calculated risk, Drake. That's using me so that you can get paid. That's fucking… exploitation, that's what that is."

Drake rose to his feet and took up a defensive posture.

"I didn't get *paid,* Chase. I did it because I had to… I had to get some evidence he had on the mayor, on Ken Smith. And without your help—"

"My help? My *help*?" Chase shouted. People had started to stare now, but she didn't care. The lack of sleep, the stress from her friend being dead and two others kidnapped, and now *this*? This utter violation of her trust? It was all too much. "I got your ass out of prison so that you can help me… little did I know that you were the one responsible for this fucking mess!"

"I'm sorry," Drake said, once again lowering his eyes. "I didn't mean or want for any this to happen. As I said, I thought he'd be locked up forever. But I'm here now, and I'm going to help you find your friends."

Chase growled like some sort of feral animal.

"I don't need your help—I don't fucking need it, and I don't want it."

Drake looked up.

"Please, Chase," he pleaded. "Let me make this right. Just let me help you."

Let me…

It was a curious choice of words, something that Chase harkened back to what Dr. Matteo used to say. It wasn't exactly the same thing, but it shared a condescending tone.

"You know what, Drake? You can go to hell." Chase turned to all of the onlookers. "All of you, all of you can just go to hell."

With that, she stormed out of the bar.

"Chase, please—Chase! *Chase!*"

Chase kept on walking.

She'd come to Drake because she thought he could be trusted.

She was wrong.

The truth was that there was only one person in this world that she could count on.

Herself.

Chase just hoped that this was enough to save her friends.

Chapter 10

For close to five minutes after Chase left, Damien Drake simply sat at the table, his eyes locked on his scotch.

Truthfully, with everything that had happened to him over the past year or so, he'd forgotten all about his dealings with Marcus Slasinsky. At the time, providing the man with Chase's personal items seemed like a small price to pay to bring down one of the most corrupt public officials in New York City history—maybe even in *US* history.

But now…

Chase had blown up and Drake didn't blame her. Once again, he'd done what he thought was right, but had neglected to even consider the collateral damage.

And she doesn't know the half of it.

He'd held back the fact that in addition to hair and other trinkets, Drake had also given the psychopath a vial of Chase's blood. A vial that Stitts had provided him.

Drake was beginning to think that his decision to leave the Virgin Gorda had been a mistake, that others would have been better off if he'd stayed away.

Maybe Chase is right, maybe everyone is better off without me.

"Fuck," he said as he finished his drink. Before he'd even placed the empty glass down on the table that was still wet with spilled beer, the bartender appeared at his side.

"Everything all right, Drake?" Mickey asked.

Drake looked up at the man's face, his bushy mustache, his dark eyes.

"No," he said simply.

"Didn't think so."

The man produced a bottle of Johnny Walker Black Label and poured him two fingers. Then he put the bottle on the table.

Drake drank the liquid in one gulp. Mickey raised an eyebrow and reached for the bottle with the intention of filling him up again.

"That bad?"

"That bad."

But when he went to pour, Drake stopped him.

"Not today, Mickey."

He rose to his feet.

The old Drake would have sat there and finished the bottle wallowing in what could have been. But he couldn't do that—Chase needed him. She might claim that she didn't, but Chase didn't always know what was best for her.

He'd returned to New York to help a friend and it had cost him his freedom. The penalty for *not* helping Chase, he feared, would be far, far worse.

Mickey put the cap on the bottle.

"It's nice to have you back," he said. This was clearly meant as a simple platitude, but Drake took it to heart.

"Yeah, well, you might be the only one."

He slipped a twenty on the table and before Mickey could protest, he started toward the door.

"Hey, Drake, where are you going?"

"To help a friend," he muttered as he pushed the door wide and stepped out into the sun. "To help a friend."

Chapter 11

CHASE WAS FUMING WHEN she left the bar. She was so angry, in fact, that when she got behind the wheel of her car, she had to take a breather before starting it in fear of running someone over.

Drake had given Marcus Slasinsky her personal possessions and had inadvertently helped him escape. And now, her friends had been kidnapped, and a man turns up murdered with a butterfly drawn in blood on his chest. It wasn't the same as the butterfly that Marcus had drawn on his victims—those had been more detailed and were on their backs—but it was all too much of a coincidence to ignore.

Stitts had taught her that much.

"Fuck!"

Chase slammed her hands down on the wheel. Then she closed her eyes and took a deep breath in through her nose, out through her mouth.

Stay in the moment, Chase. Be present.

The reality was, none of this mattered. The only thing that was important right now was finding Stitts and Louisa.

The problem was, Chase had no idea where to start. That was why she'd come to Drake in the first place. The FBI was working on trying to piece together both Louisa and Stitts' final moments before being taken, but it was up to her, on the ground in New York, to find them.

She was hoping that Drake would have some connections, maybe, or perhaps an informant of his from a past life had overheard some chatter.

It was a stretch, but it was *something*.

Or maybe they weren't the first people to be taken and Beckett had come across something important in the morgue.

But Beckett was dead.

Chase cursed again.

A year ago, she would've said that her life couldn't get any worse: addicted to heroin, desperate to find her sister, abusing her body in any way possible without a second thought about the consequence to either herself or anyone else.

But over the course of the last twenty-four hours, it was as if her life had been put into a blender and blitzed using the 'ice-crush' setting.

The goddamn chef didn't even have the common decency to put in a little seasoning.

"Fuck." This time, Chase whispered the word. She reached up and wiped tears from her eyes.

Once again, she was alone—alone, hunting a man who had taken someone close to her; two people this time.

It was like the Brian Jalston nightmare that would never end.

Chase closed her eyes as more tears started to well.

In her mind, she saw an image of her sister, but not as the cute little redhead with the button nose and freckles, but as a woman.

Fury painted Georgina's face like a hideous mask.

Chase opened her eyes and saw Drake stepping out of the bar. His hands were shoved deep into his pockets and his eyes were low. He moved with purpose.

"How could you do this?" she said softly. "How could you do this to me?"

Chase considered going to the man then. She had a feeling that despite what he'd done, she was going to need Drake's help before this was all over.

But she couldn't bring herself to do it.

Chase hadn't wanted Floyd to come with her to New York because people who got close to her—people like Louisa and Stitts—inevitably got hurt.

But the truth was, this was only part of the reason.

The other half was self-preservation; *she* didn't want to get hurt.

FBI Agent Chris Martinez had bruised Chase when she'd discovered that he wasn't her mentor, but a goddamn psychopath hell-bent on revenge. Stitts had broken her heart when he'd thrown their entire friendship away after not being able to deal with the fact that they'd slept together. And Georgina had crushed her soul the day that Chase had finally found her in the house with her 'sisters'.

She simply couldn't take any more pain and suffering. Not from Floyd.

Not from Drake.

Chase sighed as she watched Drake turn down the side of the bar and then break into a jog.

But she wasn't just going to sit here, either.

Because no matter what Chase was going through, no matter how severe her problems were, Stitts and Louisa needed her.

Dr. Matteo had once told her that if she really wanted to get better, if Chase was to truly heal, then she had to learn a new way to deal with her problems.

That meant no drugs, no sleeping around, and no throwing herself into her work.

"Well, fuck you, Dr. Matteo. My work is all I have left."

Chapter 12

WITH NO CAR, DRAKE had to walk to *SLH Investigations,* which took over an hour. Yet, when he finally got there, he didn't enter right away. Instead, he stood down the side of the building and contemplated what to do next.

He wanted to go inside and give Screech a hug, Hanna too, and shake Leroy's hand.

He also wanted to put the 'D' back on the door and make it DSLH Investigations again. Or maybe Triple D, like the good ol' days—back when things were less... *complicated.*

But dragging Leroy and Screech into this mess wasn't fair to them. Hanna, on the other hand... well, she'd been the one who'd hauled him back from the Virgin Gorda.

He got his cell phone out, which Dunbar had somehow managed to retrieve from evidence, and scrolled to a familiar number.

A female voice answered on the first ring.

"No Caller ID? If this is a telemarketer—"

"Hanna, it's Drake."

There was a pause, likely as Hanna tried to figure out if it was really him.

"You get one phone call and used it to call me? I'm flattered, but maybe you should consider calling your lawyer."

Drake ignored the comment.

"Did you hear about Beckett?"

Another pause, one that stretched on for longer than the first.

"Yeah, I'm sorry, Drake. It was fucked up... he just dropped dead, right there in the hospital. I know you two were close... no word on a funeral yet—could be a week or more before that happens. You think they're going to let you out for—"

"I'm outside now."

"*What*? What do you mean? How can you—"

"Calm down, Hanna. I need your help with something. You think you can meet me?"

"Yeah, of course. I'll be out in one second. But—"

"Don't tell Screech," Drake said calmly. "Don't tell Screech or Leroy—and bring my gun."

***

As soon as Hanna stepped out of the building, Drake leaned around the side and motioned for her to come over.

There was something akin to confusion and joy on her face, which was an odd combination. She broke into a jog and then surprised Drake by hugging him tightly. This was so out of character that it took him a moment before he hugged her back.

"Sorry about that," Hanna said, taking a step backward. "Just had to make sure it was really you. I mean, it looks like you—minus the spare tire around the middle. Drake, what the fuck is going on? How did you get out?"

Drake debated how much to tell the woman.

"It's temporary," he settled on at last. "I'm not sure how long I'm going to be free, which is why I don't want the others to know about it."

Hanna looked skyward.

"Who's after you? The mob? Cops?"

Drake started to shake his head, then reconsidered and shrugged.

"Someone's always after me. I just—I can't believe that Beckett's dead."

Hanna chewed the inside of her lip and lowered her gaze.

"Yeah, it came out of nowhere. One day he was here, the next he was gone. For the most part, the whole thing has been kept under wraps, as if someone doesn't want the public to know about it. Shit, if it hadn't been for Dunbar calling, I don't think I would have found out."

Drake scowled.

"Did Dunbar say how he died?"

"Aneurysm."

"Aneurysm?"

Drake knew that Beckett liked to party a little, which included the occasional nose-candy and expensive scotch. But he wasn't one for excess.

"Yeah, that's what Dunbar said; an aneurysm. How did *you* hear about it?"

"I went to go visit him, and the new ME told me he was dead. She's a piece of work, that one."

"Ah, Dr. Karen Cuntmeyer. Yeah, she and Beckett didn't get along too well."

The doctor's words echoed in Drake's head: *I'm not going to lie! Not after what Beckett did!*

Something was seriously wrong with this situation, beyond the obvious. The secrecy, the delayed funeral, the confusion about the cause of death… it wasn't *normal.* Not that anything with Beckett was ever normal.

Drake scratched the back of his head.

"Have you seen his body? Has *anybody* seen his body?"

"No. Screech and I tried, but they moved him to another county. Something about a conflict of interest or some bullshit."

"What county?"

"Westchester—a small morgue with an attached psych facility."

Hanna's eyes suddenly went wide.

"What? What is it?"

"Shit… you don't know, do you?"

"Know what?"

"About Suzan."

Drake's eyes narrowed. Suzan wasn't just Beckett's girlfriend, she was also the daughter of his late partner, Clay Cuthbert. Not to mention the fact that Suzan's mother, Jasmine Cuthbert, had given birth to Drake's child less than a year ago.

A child that he hadn't seen but for ten minutes since he was born.

"What about Suzan, Hanna? What are you talking about?"

Hanna took a cautious step backward.

"Hanna?"

The woman's eyebrows lifted. She was a tough woman, without whom Drake probably wouldn't be alive today. She was the one who helped him escape from Oak Valley… him and Marcus Slasinsky.

"Hanna, tell me—"

"Suzan's been institutionalized, Drake. After Beckett died, she lost her mind. Started speaking a whole lot of crazy and they locked her up because of it."

Chapter 13

CHASE STRODE INTO 62ND precinct with her badge at the ready and her head held high. She passed several uniformed officers, none of whom gave her so much as a second glance, before striding directly up to the office that she'd once occupied.

She was dismayed to find that, like Beckett's office back at NYU Med, there was no name on the door indicating the presiding sergeant. Frowning, she knocked anyway. When there was no answer, she pressed her face to the frosted glass flanking the door, but she couldn't make out anything inside.

She knocked again.

"Excuse me? Can I help you with something?"

Chase turned around, a sour expression on her face.

"Yeah, the Sergeant. I'm looking—Dunbar?"

"What—what are you doing here, Chase?" Dunbar asked as he glanced around. "I thought you and Drake..."

The man appeared nervous, and Chase knew that it wasn't fair for her to show up like this. Sure, Director Hampton had put in the call to have Drake released on bail—which had ruffled more than a few feathers—but it had been Dunbar who had gone to bat for him.

If Drake got himself into trouble, it would be Dunbar who would pay the price.

Still, Chase had a job to do.

Friends to save.

"Who's the sergeant here?"

Dunbar was confused by her sudden change in posture.

"We... we don't have one, Chase."

"What about Yasiv? Sergeant Yasiv? Where's he at? I need to speak with whoever is in charge."

Dunbar swallowed hard.

"A lot has changed since you were the sergeant, Chase. And I mean, *a lot*."

Chase thought back to her time at 62nd precinct, more than two years ago. After Sergeant Rhodes, a hothead with a mean streak who had been ousted by Drake, *she'd* been promoted to the position. That hadn't lasted long; the FBI had come calling and Chase had vacated the post. The mayor, in an attempt to quell rumors about corruption in both his ranks and the NYPD, had promoted a young, naive detective by the name of Henry Yasiv. The mayor had clearly thought that the man was someone he could influence, but Yasiv had proven a tough nut to crack.

Drake had mentioned some time ago that Yasiv was someone he trusted.

It appeared, however, that there had been another shakeup in the ranks.

Dunbar looked around, nodding at several officers who had stopped to observe their interaction with keen interest.

"Maybe… maybe we should go somewhere else and talk."

Chase checked her watch. It was coming up on eleven-thirty.

"Yeah, I think that's a good idea—so long as the place you have in mind serves alcohol. Looks like we're both going to have to get each other up to speed. And fast."

Chapter 14

THE WESTCHESTER COUNTY MEDICAL Examiner's Office couldn't have been more different than where Drake and Hanna had just come from. Rather than being embedded within a University Hospital, it was a nondescript stand-alone structure set back from a rural road. Yet, despite this serene setting, there was an occupied guard booth out front.

Unlike back at NYU Med, Drake didn't have Chase's FBI badge to lean on.

"Think we can sneak in the back?" he asked as Hanna neared the front gate and started to slow.

She just looked at him and shook her head. To his surprise, she seemed unfazed and went right up to the gate.

Drake shrugged and just let her run with it.

"Identification, please," the man in the booth asked, without even bothering to look over at them.

Hanna said nothing, and eventually, the security guard sighed and turned to look at them.

"I said, identifi—*Hanna?*"

Hanna smiled.

"Jesus, didn't expect to see you here." The man ducked his head to get a look at Drake. "Coming for a visit?"

"Something like that. Care to lift the gate?"

"Yes, of course." The man pressed a button on the console in front of him and the gate slowly started to rise. "On your way out, we should—"

Hanna popped her VW into drive, and they passed beneath the gate with only an inch or two of clearance.

"What the hell was that all about?" Drake asked as she pulled up right outside the front doors.

"Don't ask," Hanna replied as she hopped out. Drake hurried after her and they entered the building together through dual glass doors.

There was no receptionist to greet them. In fact, aside from what looked like a family viewing area off to the right, the foyer didn't have much in the way of formal organization. Drake found himself staring down a long hallway, each side of which was flanked by closed doors.

"Can I help you with something?" a man sporting a white lab coat and a thick, dark beard asked as he stepped out of one of the rooms. In one hand was a manila file folder.

Drake's eyes drifted down to the name tag on his lab coat.

Dr. Swansea.

"We're here to see Dr. Beckett Campbell," Drake said firmly. He could feel Hanna tense to his right, but she'd done her part getting them inside.

This was Drake's domain now.

"I'm sorry, but we have yet to release Dr. Campbell's body." The man looked over his shoulder as he spoke, either for support or for security.

"We're friends of his, and we would like to see his body," Drake stated.

He stuck out his hand, but instead of shaking it, Dr. Swansea took a step backward.

"The name's Damien Drake."

This elicited no outward response.

"I'm sorry, but there's nothing I can do. You need to leave now."

What the fuck is going on here?

"No, I'm sorry that you seem to have misunderstood. We *are* going to see—"

"Please, excuse my friend," Hanna interrupted as she stepped in front of Drake. "He's been away, and his social graces aren't what they should be. We were both shocked to hear the news of Beckett's passing, and would really appreciate if we could see his body. You know, for closure? I swear, we'll only be a minute."

Dr. Swansea's face softened for a moment, giving Drake hope that Hanna's approach would prove fruitful.

He was disappointed.

"You can't see him—I'm sorry." Dr. Swansea shook his head. "Now, please, I'll ask you again to leave and then I'll call the police."

Drake felt his blood pressure start to rise.

"What about Suzan?" He snapped. "Can I see Suzan Cuthbert?"

Dr. Swansea's frown suddenly became a scowl.

"I can't discuss patients."

"That's what she is? A patient?" Drake looked around. "Is she here? Or somewhere else?"

Dr. Swansea started to reach for the phone clipped to his hip. "Please leave now."

Drake sized the doctor up. He was of an average build, with dark eyes that matched his beard. It was clear that this wasn't your typical Point Dexter-type GP, but that didn't matter, because Drake wasn't your average PI.

"Tell me where Suzan is," he repeated.

"Dr. Swansea? Everything okay?" a man who poked his head out of one of the many rooms asked.

"Everything's fine—these people were just—"

Drake's right arm shot out and his fingers wrapped around Dr. Swansea's throat. The man immediately grabbed at his hand, but Drake held fast. Within seconds, Dr. Swansea's face started to turn red and he began to wheeze.

"Tell me where the fuck Suzan Cuthbert is," he demanded.

"Drake," Hanna hissed. Her hands joined Dr. Swansea's in a combined attempt to get him to stop choking the doctor.

Drake responded by squeezing even harder and stared into the man's dark irises.

"Where the fuck is she?"

Dr. Swansea tried to speak, but the only thing he could manage was an incoherent gasp and some spit.

"Tell me—"

A sharp pain in his side finally broke the trance. Drake looked down and saw that Hanna was pinching him just above his hip. It was a superficial affront, but his liver had been through much damage over the years, and the muscles on that side of his body contracted protectively.

He let go of the man's throat. Dr. Swansea immediately started to cough and rub at the red marks below his beard.

"We gotta get out of here, Drake," Hanna said, her eyes going wide.

Squinting, Drake looked around. It wasn't just the man from one of the side rooms who had taken notice of this exchange now, but a half-dozen doctors, some of whom had their phones pressed to their ears. From the expressions on their faces, it was obvious that they weren't calling to renew their Yankee season tickets.

"Yeah, I think that's a good idea," Drake whispered as he started to back up. Getting arrested again wouldn't help Suzan at all… or Chase.

It wouldn't help anyone, himself included.

Dr. Swansea, who was still rubbing his throat, leveled his eyes at Drake.

"You're going to be sorry you did that," the man said in a voice so low that Drake had to strain to hear. "If you're not careful, you're going to find your name on a card one day, Damien Drake."

Hanna was pulling him backward now, and he tried to stop.

"Fuck did you just say?"

"Drake, let's go!" Hanna said with a tug.

Drake relented and allowed himself to be pulled out the front doors, but he never broke Dr. Swansea's stare.

"Did you hear that? Hanna, did you—"

"Come on, let's get the fuck out here." She spun him around and shoved him toward her car. Once inside the vehicle, Hanna turned to face him. "What the fuck was that, Drake? What the *fuck*?"

Drake shut his eyes. When he saw his brother's face and the bullet hole in the center of his forehead, he opened them again.

"Nothing. Let's just go before I decide to ask Dr. Swansea to clarify what he meant back there."

Chapter 15

"I DON'T... I DON'T even know what to say," Chase grumbled. Her life after leaving the NYPD had been a hot mess, but it appeared as if the NYPD itself had caught whatever disease affected her.

Sergeant Yasiv going all-in on Beckett being a murderer, then he himself being charged with a double homicide by the DA?

What in the fuck is going on here?

"Tell me about it," Dunbar said as he averted his eyes and took a sip of beer. "Without you and Drake... well, things just haven't been right around here."

And now that we're back? We're not a panacea, Dunbar; if anything, Drake and I are like an opportunistic infection that is destined to cripple this once great city.

She shook her head.

"So, no sergeant at all?"

"Not for now, anyway. DA Trumbo is running the show, and it looks like he's going to toss his hat into the ring for the vacant mayor spot. Listen, I don't mind catching up, but this whole surprise visit and getting Drake released on 'bail'... and then you come here looking for a sergeant?" Dunbar sighed. "You know, I trust Drake—I do. But after Yasiv went AWOL, I'm not just on a fucking limb here, but I'm sitting on one of its weak-ass spindly branches, you know? And there's someone sawing at the place where it meets the tree."

Chase stared at the man as he spoke. She remembered him when he was green and naive; both she and Drake had thought that becoming Detective was out of the question for Dunbar. Evidently, he'd proven them both wrong.

But this hadn't come without a price; it weighed heavily on the man.

She could see it in his eyes, the way his shoulders drooped. And while Chase was averse to getting anyone else involved in this situation, she really needed someone on her team.

"I'm looking for a few friends. Friends who were taken."

Dunbar nearly coughed up some beer.

"*Taken*? You mean, like, *kidnapped?*"

Chase swallowed hard and nodded.

"Shit, Chase, how can I help? I can set up a task force… Jesus, are they *here*? In New York? What's—" the man was struggling to find the words. Clearly, this wasn't what he'd been expecting. "What can I do?"

"I… I don't know," Chase conceded. "Two of my friends were taken from Virginia and then somehow brought to New York. Got a photo of them—it wasn't pretty. That's why I'm here, Dunbar. I have people back at Quantico trying to trace the call, as well as my friends' last movements, but so far we've hit a dead end."

"And Drake? Where's he?"

Chase looked away.

"He's tracking down some other leads. I tried to get Beckett—fuck, is he really dead?"

"Yeah," Dunbar said dryly. "He was a good man. Weird as hell, but good—dependable. Yasiv had it all wrong about him…"

Chase pictured Beckett with the bloody stone in his hand.

Was he? Was Yasiv wrong about Beckett? And did it even matter now that he's gone?

"I don't—I can't even process that right now. We went to the morgue to find him but just got the runaround. We did, however, find a murdered young man with his face painted and a butterfly on his chest. Know anything about that?"

Dunbar leaned forward in his chair.

"Michael Brian; farmhand found murdered in a field not a hundred yards from his place."

"The butterfly… remember Marcus Slasinsky, or Dr. Mark Kruk as he was known professionally?"

"Yeah, I think so—guy spent years in a psych facility after being tormented as a child, but then rebuilt his life. Even become a psychiatrist, all just to seek revenge against the bullies who ruined his childhood. Twisted case—would have made a great book, if you're into that sort of thing. Just started in the NYPD when you and Drake were hunting for the man. What about—wait, you think that this might be related to Marcus Slasinsky?"

Chase cocked her head to one side.

"Not sure—Drake thinks so. Also told me that he—" she cleared her throat, "—that Marcus somehow managed to escape from Oak Valley."

Dunbar snapped his fingers.

"Shit, you know what? You're right. Not only that, but it was…" Dunbar swallowed hard and let his sentence trail off.

But it was Drake who helped him get out.

Under normal circumstances, Chase would have been appalled at the idea that a Detective in the NYPD had forgotten about a serial killer's escape… a mentally deranged one, at that. But Dunbar had already given her a rundown of the events since she'd left the NYPD, and, sad as it was, Marcus Slasinsky's breakout was hardly front-page news.

Not while the mayor was being accused of running a sex trafficking and heroin distribution ring.

Besides, she knew that Hanna and Drake were responsible for Marcus' escape, and it was in the NYPD's best interest—*their* best interest, anyway—for this to remain relatively quiet.

Dunbar must have noticed her change in expression because he suddenly started trying to justify his poor memory.

"The DA? He tried to bury that whole Marcus Slasinsky thing. Come to think of it, he's trying to keep the press out of *all* police business. Looks bad for him and his mayoral bid. I mean, just look at this Mike Brian case. DA already came down and asked us to wrap it up quick, and you know what that means."

Chase nodded.

"A nobody farmer? Close the case or ship it somewhere else—cold case, even."

"Yeah. And this Mike Brian was no saint, either, which doesn't help. Multiple arrests and even a short stint in Riker's for armed robbery."

Chase hated that politics were involved in the NYPD, in police work in general, but the reality was, with limited resources, cases had to be prioritized. And the murder of an ex-con wasn't usually high on the totem pole.

Unless it could be linked to other cases, that is.

"Any suspects? Any idea what this face paint thing is all about?"

Dunbar shook his head.

"No—like I said, there's only one Detective working the case. All I know is that Mike Brian wasn't shy about calling out gays and queers—twice he was arrested for random attacks during the Pride Parade. Maybe it was somebody's idea of a cruel joke after killing him? You know, turn him into a transvestite or something? But… Chase, the butterfly? You think it might be Marcus? The Butterfly Killer?"

Chase wasn't sure she liked the excited quality in Dunbar's voice.

"Maybe—I'll know more in a few minutes."

Dunbar looked confused.

"A few minutes? What's going to happen then?"

"Then I'll be able to process everything you're about to tell me about Marcus Slasinsky, before and after his escape."

Chapter 16

"YOU REALLY THINK ALL this is related to Marcus Slasinsky? You think that he's responsible for kidnapping Chase's partner and friend?" Hanna asked as she pulled into the back lot of Oak Valley Psychiatric Facility. "Better yet, do you think we can actually get in there without them locking both of us up?"

Drake glanced up at the brown building and immediately felt a pang deep in the pit of his stomach. The last time he'd been here it had been as a patient. Sure, he'd orchestrated the entire thing so that Hanna, who worked there at the time, could help him escape, but being alone with his thoughts for even that long was a nightmare-inducing experience.

He shuddered.

"I—I don't know," Drake said at last. When he'd first seen the butterfly painted on the corpse's chest back in the morgue, he'd immediately associated it with Marcus. But that wasn't surprising given the fact that ever since he'd nearly put a bullet between the man's eyes, every butterfly he saw reminded Drake of Marcus Slasinsky.

But the whole face painting? The white face and red lips? It didn't fit the man's MO.

Not in the least.

Realizing that Hanna was staring at him, Drake shrugged.

"That's all I got."

She made a face.

"That's all you got? You stare off into space like some sort of zombie for half an hour, and the best you can come up with is 'that's all I got?' Shit, you might have changed, Drake, but your communication skills still need some work."

"Sorry I'm not more of a Chatty Kathy."

Hanna blinked.

"Chatty Kathy? Jesus, you really are forty going on ninety, you know that? Anyways, if we're going to do this, let's fucking do it. This time, please, *please,* just let me do the talking. And for fuck's sake, no rape choking… got it?"

***

The closer that Drake got to the rear doors of Oak Valley Psychiatric Facility, the more his heart started to race. And when Hanna knocked on the door in a specific pattern, he reached for her arm. He intended on telling her that this was a bad idea when the door suddenly started to open.

Drake leaped backward and prepared to run.

Hanna, on the other hand, was all in.

"Where's Dorian or Dr. Pritchard? I need to speak to them immediately," she ordered in a tone that Drake barely recognized.

The man who peered out was tall and thin, with a narrow nose and dirty blond hair cut close to his scalp. He was wearing a white lab coat, but there was no name tag visible.

Drake didn't recognize the man from his time here, but that wasn't surprising given his relatively short stay.

"Excuse—excuse me?"

Hanna grabbed the door and pulled it wide. The man, clearly startled, moved out of the way. When Drake just stood in the parking lot, Hanna gestured for him to enter.

"I need to speak to either Dorian or Dr. Pritchard. Are either of them in?"

"I—I—Dr. Pritchard is here, but I'm afraid that Dorian is on leave for the next week or so. And you are…?"

Hanna once again indicated for Drake to enter, this time more desperately, and he obliged, only to immediately regret his decision.

The harsh incandescent lighting, the smell of stale air, and the claustrophobic closeness of the walls all served to incite near panic in Drake.

"It doesn't matter who I am. Dr. Pritchard will know who I am. Take me to him."

The man in the lab coat looked her up and down, then turned to Drake who couldn't hold his gaze.

It can't really be this easy, can it?

Hanna was something of a chameleon, able to seamlessly become anyone she needed to—and she used to work here—but Oak Valley was home to some of the most dangerous criminals in New York.

Drake half-expected the lanky doctor to either call security immediately or tell them to go fuck themselves.

He did neither.

"Come with me—I'll take you to Dr. Pritchard."

Hanna offered a single nod and then held her hand out, letting the doctor lead the way.

"What's your name?" she asked, falling into stride beside him. Drake took up the rear, each step more hesitant than the previous.

"Glenn—I just started here a few weeks ago."

Drake listened with half an ear as they moved down the hallway. He was distracted by the thick blue doors that marked the entrance to each cell. Through the inlayed shatterproof window, he could see the white walls, the mattress on the floor.

If you weren't crazy when you were admitted, it was only a matter of time...

As they continued to walk, Drake was struck by just how empty the place was. He recalled how loud everything had been when he'd first come here as a patient. Even though the rooms were designed to be soundproof, there was a limit to how much they could actually block out. This paradoxically made the experience even more unnerving, like straining to understand someone speaking underwater.

But not today.

Today, Oak Valley was suspiciously calm.

"Where is everyone?" Drake asked.

Hanna shot him a look, but Glenn didn't seem perturbed by the query.

"I'm afraid that it's not been the same since you were here." Glenn strode forward and then indicated the second of two adjacent doors that were open into the hallway. "Dr. Pritchard's in there."

Hanna doubled down on her authoritative posture and moved to the front of the door and peered inside.

I'm afraid that it's not been the same since you were here.

The comment gave Drake pause.

"How long did you say you've worked here for again?" he asked.

Glenn looked around and then offered him a strange smile.

"Oh, not long. Not long at all."

Drake frowned but before he could press the man further, Hanna pulled her head out from behind the open door.

"Is this some kind of joke? He's not—"

Glenn shot forward with incredible speed. Before Drake could even bring his hand to the holster on his hip, the man's arms seemed to stretch like putty. He shoved Hanna in the back, and she stumbled into the cell. She cried out, but Glenn slammed the door closed with his foot, immediately muffling the sound.

"Hey!" Drake shouted.

Glenn spun around, leading with something long and thin that glinted in the harsh lighting. Drake tried to parry the attack, even went as far as to throw both hands up and tried to suck in his stomach, but the blade sliced through his t-shirt just beneath his right arm and drew blood.

"You mother—"

Glenn continued to spin like some sort of human dreidel, his long, spindly arms shoving Drake once, twice, and then a third time before he could even catch his bearings.

Just as he managed to pull his gun free, Drake found himself inside the second cell with the door slammed closed.

He immediately aimed his pistol at the glass, but somehow resisted the urge to pull the trigger, which would have only served to deafen him and dent the thick partition.

In the window, Glenn stared back, his eyes wide, a huge grin on his face.

Then the man waved and vanished.

Chapter 17

"**AFTER WHAT HAPPENED WITH** Drake and Hanna, Marcus Slasinsky disappeared. We put out a BOLO, tagged his name for any credit or bank applications, including all known aliases, and flagged his fingerprints. So far as I know, there's been zero activity, and that was more than three months ago. My guess? He's gone—fled into Mexico or up into Canada."

This made sense if Marcus Slasinsky was your run of the mill criminal. Hell, it might even be true of Marcus Slasinsky, but there was something else that needed to be considered: the man's split-personality, Dr. Mark Kruk. The psychiatrist had extensive training and experience in understanding the human psyche. If anyone could find a way to disappear, to adopt a new persona while they plotted their revenge, it was Dr. Kruk.

"Maybe... what happened to the psych facility? Oak Valley?"

Dunbar shrugged.

"The DA paid lip service by shuttling most patients to other facilities while he 'reviewed the security protocols' or some bullshit—I don't think he did anything substantial, though. As far as I know, it's still open, but only houses a handful of patients."

Chase bit her bottom lip as she considered how to continue.

"I want to go there."

Dunbar sipped his beer.

"Sure, I can take you, but if you want to speak to patients, I doubt—" Dunbar's brow suddenly furrowed, and his eyes drifted over Chase's shoulder. "Can I help you with something?"

"I'm-I'm here to see Chase."

Chase instantly recognized the man's voice and spun around in her chair so quickly that she nearly fell off it.

"Floyd?" Chase jumped to her feet. "What the hell are you doing here? I told Director—" she stopped speaking when she saw the expression on the man's face. "What's wrong? Did you find them? Fuck. Tell me they're not dead, Floyd. Please, tell me—"

Floyd gaped and he held up a briefcase.

"Oh, no, God no—nothing like that. I just—Chase I've got something that you need to see."

Chase exhaled loudly and she fell back into her chair.

"Jesus… Floyd, I told Director Hampton—"

"I know, I know. But that was before… that was before—"

"I'm sorry, but who are you?" Dunbar asked.

Floyd took this as an invitation to sit and then immediately pulled a laptop out of the briefcase and started to boot it up.

"Floyd Montgomery, FBI," he said without looking up from the keyboard.

Chase, frustrated by the fact that Floyd was here, as well as his out of character cryptic behavior, lashed out.

"What the hell are you doing here, Floyd?"

Her breathing had yet to return to normal after thinking the worst, and the words came out more angrily than she'd intended.

Floyd tore his eyes away from his computer and then looked at Dunbar.

"Maybe we should—"

"This is Detective Dunbar," she hesitated. "You can trust him."

Floyd swallowed hard and then lowered his voice.

"I had to come here—I was gonna just call you and tell you about the blood, but then we found the video and—"

Chase squeezed her eyes tightly and shook her head.

"The blood? The video? Floyd, for fuck's sake."

"Your blood was entered into NDIS, Chase. All FBI Agents have their DNA stored in the system in case—in case—"

Chase's eyes snapped open.

"*My* blood? What? By whom? Where?"

"An ME here in New York. Something to do with a murdered man? Apparently, she swabbed blood found on his chest and…"

Floyd kept on talking, but Chase didn't hear a single word of it.

Drake was right… it's happening again.

She gripped the sides of the table for support.

"Chase? You okay?" Dunbar asked, placing a hand on her back. Chase took three deep breaths and then shrugged him off.

"The bloody butterfly," she whispered. "Dr. Karen Nordmeyer ran it through the system, and it came back as mine."

"Yeah—as soon as it was entered into the system, we were notified. I brought it to Director Hampton and that's when he showed me the video."

Chase was still reeling from the first revelation and wasn't sure if she could handle another.

Drake might have been right about the link between Marcus Slasinsky and Mike Brian, and more than likely Stitts and Louisa, but he was also a lying piece of shit.

He hadn't just given Marcus 'trinkets' of hers, he'd given the psycho her blood. Her fucking *blood.*

"Why would he do that," she whispered, shaking her head. "Why would he—"

"Who? I'm not sure I'm following here," a confused sounding Dunbar inquired.

"Drake—he's... fuck, never mind." Chase looked over at Floyd. "What's this video? Is it of Mike Brian?"

If Floyd had resembled a spooked cat a few moments ago, he now looked absolutely terrified.

"Please, Floyd, just tell me what you found."

"I-I-I can't," Floyd stuttered. The man had nearly lost his stutter the last time Chase had seen him, and the fact that it had returned was alarming. "It's b-b-better if I sh-sh-sh-show you."

Chase hated the suspense but knew that getting Floyd to try and articulate his thoughts at this moment would likely take forever.

"Fine, show me," she said, moving her chair to get a better view of his laptop.

Floyd clicked a few buttons and then a video started to play. Chase squinted, trying to make sense of what she was seeing. It appeared as if Stitts was walking out of a crowded bar, his gait clearly indicating that he was intoxicated. A man and a woman flanked him on either side, and the former appeared to have his arm around Stitts' waist.

"Is this from the night he went missing?"

"Y-y-yes. We don't know who the m-m-man is, but I think you kn-kn-know the wo-wo-wo-wo-woman."

Chase's upper lip curled.

"I *know* her? Is it Louisa? No, Louisa's heavier than that. Is it—"

Floyd rewound the video and pressed play again.

"It's—it's—it's—" Floyd took a deep, hitching breath and then paused for a second before trying again. "It's your sister, Chase. Your sister took Stitts."

PART II - Breadcrumbs

Chapter 18

FBI Special Agent Jeremy Stitts rubbed his cheek vigorously on his shoulder. Eventually, the corner of the tape that covered his mouth started to peel away. When his face became sore, he attacked the tape from the inside, using his tongue to try and first moisten the glue before pressing hard against it.

He alternated between these two approaches for a full five minutes until his tongue ached and his cheek started to blister. Just as he was about to give up, he felt the tape start to loosen and he redoubled his efforts. As he worked, Stitts kept his eyes locked on Louisa who was strapped to the chair beside him, her head tilted backward. Every so often she would moan, but her eyes never opened.

Louisa's state had deteriorated over the past twenty-four hours. She hadn't eaten, hadn't gone to the bathroom, hadn't spoken. Aside from the slow rise and fall of her chest, the only other movement came from her eyes: they fluttered in time with the frantic butterflies trapped in the massive glass enclosure behind them.

Stitts gave her another few hours, tops. She was a tough woman, that much was undeniable, but being taken and trapped in this dirt-covered basement only God knows where was simply too much for her to bear.

It was far too similar to her past, her childhood, and something inside Louisa had broken.

Their captors must have realized this as well, as her bindings—the ropes that tied her hands behind her back, as well as the ones that fastened her ankles to the wooden chair legs—were much looser than his own.

For once, neither Marcus Slasinsky nor Riley Jalston—or Georgina Adams, as Stitts knew her—were down in the basement with them. To this point, they'd alternated standing guard, but Marcus had received a call or a text and had gestured for Riley to follow him upstairs.

That had been an hour or so ago… or so Stitts thought; it was nearly impossible to judge the passage of time locked in a dungeon. Yet, he was cognizant enough to know that this was likely their only chance to escape.

As he continued to try and remove the tape from his mouth, a rat scurried across the dirt-covered floor and took up residence in front of Stitts' bare left foot.

He stopped working and tried to shoo the rodent away with his foot. All this served was to remind him of the rope burns on his ankles from previous attempts to break free.

The rat was predictably undeterred by his grunts and stared up at Stitts with beady black eyes. It was impossible for the animal to feel pity, of course, but Stitts could have sworn that was exactly what he saw in the rat's twitching face.

He was suddenly reminded of Piper, the mostly retired cadaver dog who had been instrumental in him finding Lance O'Neill and saving Chase's life.

I wonder if she survived?

Piper had taken a bullet from Lance, but Stitts had fled New Mexico before finding out if she'd pulled through.

If she's alive out there, maybe I can give her a home.

It was a strange thought, but somehow reassuring.

Finding out if Piper was alive meant that *he* was still amongst the living, that Stitts had somehow broken free and fled his captors.

With a final thrust from his aching tongue, the tape suddenly peeled free.

In what was a near orgasmic gasp, Stitts inhaled deeply through his mouth. The air was hot and stale and reeked of earth and urine, but it was satisfying nonetheless.

He hissed, and the rat bolted, heading back into one of the dark corners of the boiler room or wherever they were.

Stitts turned to his fellow captive next.

"Louisa," he whispered.

The woman moaned and her head rolled in his direction, but her eyes didn't open.

"Louisa!"

The woman fell completely still.

Stitts cursed and looked around. Aside from the glass enclosure filled with butterflies, the remainder of the eight by eight-foot room had long since been neglected. The cinder block walls were crumbling in spots, and overgrown vegetation had claimed the openings.

Directly in front of his chair was the landing of a rotting staircase, at the top of which sat an equally decaying door.

If I can somehow get up there, I can just kick the fucking thing open!

But *he* couldn't get up there; Stitts' bindings were far too tight to break free of. Louisa's, on the other hand…

"Louisa, wake up!"

To his surprise, Louisa responded to his command and her eyes slowly opened.

"It's me, Agent Stitts—Chase's partner. You remember Chase, right? Of course, you do. Listen, we need to get the fuck out of here. Can you move your legs? Can you free your arms?"

The woman just stared blankly at him.

"Your bindings are looser than mine, especially the ones around your ankles. Try to kick free."

The woman did not oblige, but her eyes drifted down to Stitts' own blistered ankles.

"Yeah, yeah, your legs. Try to straighten your legs."

Louisa's eyes rolled back, and her head lolled.

"No—Louisa, no! You need to stay awake. You have to—"

The door at the top of the staircase started to open and panic set in.

Eyes wide, Stitts fell silent as he watched two figures start their descent.

There was but a single bulb in the center of the room, affixed to a warped wooden floor joist. The weak yellow light it emitted was insufficient to illuminate the faces of the people that moved toward him.

But that didn't matter; Stitts knew exactly who they were.

"Let us go," he growled. "Let us go."

A man's face suddenly came into view.

"Soon, Agent Stitts—soon."

"Let us go!" Stitts roared.

The man smiled.

"As soon as *she* gets here, we'll let you go. It's all part of the plan, Jeremy. But these things… well, they take time. And I had a lot of time to make sure that *eeeeverything* is just perfect."

The *she* who the man was referring to was Chase, of course.

It was all about Chase. Everything that had happened leading up to Stitts meeting these two at the bar, and perhaps even long before that, was about her.

Because, for reasons that Stitts didn't completely understand, Chase was the final piece in the man's twisted revenge or perverted idea of justice.

"We don't need him alive," the woman said in a southern drawl.

Stitts' entire body tensed.

"Just let us go! For fuck's sake, Georgina, Chase is your sister!"

The woman finally stepped into view. She was pretty, with short, orange-red hair and a small, slightly upturned nose.

Stitts knew better than to be drawn in by her innocent appearance. The woman had a mean streak in her, one that he'd witnessed firsthand.

"I've told you before, my name is Riley."

"No, no, it's not! It's Georgina Adams!"

The woman scowled and turned away from him.

"We don't need them alive—you already sent the picture; your little plan is in motion. Now it's my turn—Chase took everything from me, and now I'm going to take everything from her."

"Not yet," the man replied in a calm voice. "Not quite yet. But your time for revenge will come."

With that, Marcus reached out and reapplied the tape to Stitts' mouth. He tried to turn away, but Riley held his head fast. As if this wasn't enough, a second piece of tape was applied over top of the first, making it nearly impossible to breathe.

Stitts lost it and started to buck wildly in his wooden chair, but it was no use.

They might not kill him now, but they would soon.

After they dealt with Chase.

Chapter 19

CHASE WATCHED IN HORROR as Floyd played the video for the fifth time.

Her mind was telling her that this was her sister, that it was Georgina Adams or Riley Jalston or whatever she went by, but she just couldn't believe it.

Georgina's hair was shorter than it had been in Franklin, Tennessee, and she seemed slimmer, too, but it was her.

But it *wasn't*.

Because her sister couldn't be involved with Marcus, couldn't be the one responsible for taking Stitts and Louisa.

It simply wasn't possible.

"Play it again," she whispered.

"Chase, it's—" Dunbar began, but Chase interrupted.

"Floyd, play the fucking video again."

Floyd stared at her for a moment before obliging.

This time, Chase leaned in close as if more detail would prove that it wasn't Georgina.

"Is that really your sister?" Dunbar asked softly when the video ended.

Chase thought about denying it, but with Floyd looking at her with a sympathetic expression on his young face, she had no choice.

"He took her, too," she whispered. Chase wasn't sure where this idea came from, but once it left her mouth, it had become intractable. "He took her—Marcus Slasinsky took Georgina."

Dunbar leaned away from her and just stared.

"What? It's the only thing that makes sense. He took her, drugged her—I don't fucking know—indoctrinated her like Brian did way back when."

Chase paused, almost daring either Dunbar or Floyd to challenge her on this.

Neither of them did.

She nodded, which served to further cement this idea in her head.

"Who's seen this, Floyd?" Chase grabbed her drink and took a sip. "Who's seen this video?"

"Just us and Director Hampton. That's it."

"Good," Chase said with a nod. "Let's keep it that way."

"Anyone want to fill me in here?" Dunbar asked.

Chase reached out and tapped the still image of the man holding Stitts upright.

"Drake was right—this here is Marcus Slasinsky, better known as the butterfly killer. He's the one who took Stitts, Louisa... and Georgina, my sister. We find him, and we find *them*."

Dunbar looked at Floyd, clearly apprehensive. Floyd's eyes darted to her, then he nodded.

"This is the last sighting we have. Still working on Louisa, but she was at home after a meeting with her therapist."

"If we find Marcus, we'll find Stitts, Louisa, and Georgina," Chase reiterated.

Dunbar finally seemed as if he was on board.

"How does Mike Brian fit into this thing?" he asked.

Chase thought about this for a moment.

"He killed Mike to call me out."

"Yeah, the butterfly makes sense, then, but what about the makeup? I don't remember his MO, exactly, but I'm pretty sure that there was no makeup involved."

"Don't know," Chase replied sharply. "I don't know."

Dunbar rocked his head from side to side.

"I have one detective on that case, I can beef it up. Put a whole team behind it. I'll pressure—"

Chase shook her head.

"No, no, I don't think that's a good idea. If the press catches wind of this, Marcus might snap, kill them all and go back into hiding for another two years. I—*we*—can't risk it. We need to keep this small, only let people we trust in."

Dunbar clearly was uncomfortable with this, but it was Floyd who challenged her with his eyes.

"What, Floyd? What is it?"

Chase's fingers started to tingle, and she grimaced as she shook her hands out, trying to force the sensation away.

"What would St-St-Stitts do?"

Chase frowned.

"Excuse me?"

To her surprise, Floyd didn't back down. This was a very different man from the one she'd met in Alaska.

"I said, what would Stitts do? I mean, he sure as heck hated interdisciplinary teams, but what about just the FBI?" He glanced over at Dunbar. "No offense, but Stitts was taken in Virginia and the photo you received was sent from here in New York, across st-state lines, which makes this an FBI case. What about just getting a big FBI t-t-team together? I think that's what Stitts would do."

Chase shook her head the entire time that Floyd was speaking.

"No, no. As I said, we know that Marcus is capable of murder. We can't risk him knowing that we're on to him."

Floyd made a face.

"Chase, you said it yourself, he's trying to lure you out. He's c-calling to you. What does it matter if he knows we're looking for him?"

"I—I can't risk it."

Another impasse.

"You sure that's what this is about?" Floyd asked.

Chase straightened.

"What do you mean? What else would this be about?"

Floyd looked as if he was about to say something, but instead bit his tongue.

"Spit it out, Floyd. We don't have time for these games."

Floyd's shoulders sagged.

"I just want to make sure that you're being ra-rational."

Chase suddenly exploded.

"Rational? You want me to be rational? Really? My sister, my partner, and my best friend are being held captive by a psychopath, and you want me to be *rational*? I've dealt with Marcus Slasinsky before, Floyd. I *know* him. I will catch this motherfucker, but we're going to do it *my* way. You got that?"

"Calm down," Dunbar suggested. His eyes were darting about the room, suggesting to Chase that others had taken notice. She didn't care.

"I will not fucking calm down. Don't *tell* me to calm down. I'm not—you know what?" Chase threw her hands up. "You guys stay the fuck out of my case. I started this alone, and I'll end it alone."

With that, Chase stormed out from the bar, daring any and all of the other patrons to say something—*anything*—to her.

I don't care what they think—Georgina is a victim here. Marcus has brainwashed her, and he'll kill her, along with Stitts and Louisa—unless I find him first.

Chase walked briskly to her BMW.

And after I find him, I'm going to kill the bastard. I'm going to put a bullet in Marcus Slasinsky's head like Drake should have done all those years ago.

Chapter 20

DRAKE WAS FURIOUS AT himself. He knew that something was up the minute that the tall bastard had opened the door and let them inside.

After multiple escapes, including one less than six months ago involving a serial killer, security should have been tighter than Fort Knox.

Only worked here for a little while, my ass.

He had no idea who this Glenn bastard was, if he was even a doctor or a patient or someone completely unrelated, but that didn't matter now.

Now, he was locked in a cell, with his stomach covered in blood. He'd since removed his shirt and inspected the wound; thankfully, it seemed superficial, but rather than comfort him, this only added to Drake's anger.

I should've fought harder; I should've never fallen for this shit.

As these thoughts paraded through his mind, Drake adjusted his grip on the gun in his hand.

If Glenn comes back, this time I won't hesitate to use it.

He also had his phone, but there was no signal inside the cell—he knew from experience that nearly the entire building was a dead zone, a precaution in case any patient managed to smuggle or steal a communication device.

"Open the fucking door, Glenn!" he shouted. To emphasize his words, which he knew that Glenn couldn't understand even if he was standing just on the other side, Drake banged on the door with the heel of his hand. "Open up!"

He was surprised that a response actually came. Only, it wasn't from Glenn, but Hanna in the adjacent cell.

Or maybe it was just his thoughts; both were equally as incoherent now.

"Open up!"

Drake's throat was hoarse, and his hand hurt from hitting the door, but he kept it up, if only to drown out the voices in his head.

The last time he'd been in a cell like this one, he'd nearly been driven insane. It didn't help that the only person he'd talked to was the very person he'd come here looking for: Marcus Slasinsky.

"Open the fucking door!"

More muffled replies, which Drake ascertained was more than likely Hanna's doing this time. That was good; that meant that Glenn hadn't killed her yet.

"Hey! Hey, Glenn! I'm the one you want!"

Drake kicked the door until he was sweating and the blood from the knife gash had soaked the waistband of his jeans.

Eventually, he gave up and retreated to the back wall of the cell. There, he curled into a ball and pressed his knees to his chest.

His mind instantly began to wander, to take him back to a place he didn't want to visit.

"Just leave me alone," he whined.

Drake was back in the Columbian jungle, aiming a gun at his brother's head.

"Please."

As he started to whimper, more blood leaked from his wound. Drake pulled his face out of his knees and stared down at it as a way to center himself. The gash was indeed superficial, but it was also long, about ten inches long, stretching from his navel to beneath his right arm.

Something suddenly clicked in Drake's brain.

It was a familiar wound, one of several that he'd seen earlier that morning with Chase.

Except they weren't on his abdomen, but on the stomach of a man whose face was covered in some sort of transvestite mask.

A man who also happened to have a bloody butterfly scrawled on his chest.

Chapter 21

"SORRY, CHASE, BUT WE'RE not moving," Dunbar said. Floyd nodded, confirming that they were both determined to stand directly in front of her car.

Chase's upper lip curled. She considered putting the car into drive, not to run them over, but to scare them a little. It was this transient thought that quelled some of her anger.

Get a grip—these are your friends, Chase. In the moment.

"You may have started this thing on your own, but we won't let it end that way," Floyd stated without even a hint of a stutter.

Chase leaned out of her window and observed the two men.

They cared about her, that had never been in question. But they had to do it her way; she had to make sure that Georgina was protected, that nothing happened to her.

Or Stitts or Louisa. Don't forget about them.

"We won't move, Chase," Dunbar continued, crossing his arms over his chest. "No matter what you—"

"Oh, shut the fuck up and get in the car, then. We're just wasting time here."

***

"You sure this is the place?" Chase asked as she pulled up to the front gates of Oak Valley Psychiatric Facility.

"Yeah, positive," Dunbar replied from the passenger seat.

"Looks empty," Floyd offered from the back.

"Yeah, but why?"

Chase slowed as she neared the security booth only to drive right past when she saw that it was unmanned.

"As I said earlier, most of the patients were moved to other facilities after the whole Marcus Slasinsky episode."

"Yeah, but you'd think that there would be *some* fucking security," Chase grumbled. "Given the fact that this place houses some dangerous psychos."

There were only four other cars in the lot: a camel-colored sedan, two dark hybrid vehicles, and a blue Volkswagen.

"At least someone's here."

As if on cue, a man in a white coat stepped out of the front doors. When he spotted them, his eyes went wide.

Chase was the first one out of the car.

"Chase Adams, FBI," she said flashing her badge.

It was almost as if the man didn't believe her; he took her badge and scanned it closely. Despite his extraordinary height, there was something feminine about his features. It didn't look as if he'd shaved recently, yet Chase couldn't detect any stubble.

With a frown, the doctor returned her badge. There was some sort of white powder on the back and Chase wiped it off on her pants before slipping it back into her pocket.

"You have an appointment?" he asked in a gravelly voice.

"No, we're just here to speak to your security guy."

The man nodded.

"Just inside the door, beside reception. Wait there and someone should help you in a minute or two. Now, if you'll excuse me, I just finished my shift and need to get going."

Chase moved aside and the man pulled a set of keys from his pocket. She watched him make his way to the camel-colored car and couldn't help but wonder what in the world would inspire a man, a doctor with money, to drive such an ugly vehicle. As if sensing her stare, before he got in, the man looked over the hood at her.

"I'll be seeing you, Chase."

Chase looked to Dunbar and then Floyd, who had since joined her in the parking lot.

"What the fuck was that all about?"

Floyd shrugged and Dunbar made a face.

"Fuck it, let's just get inside, see if we can pull that footage of Marcus Slasinsky while he was a patient here. Hopefully, there's something that can give us an idea of where he might have taken our friends."

They walked toward the front doors, but with every step, the doctor's final words—*I'll be seeing you, Chase*—weighed on her. Just before stepping inside, she turned back once more. The camel-colored car appeared to be idling near the security booth. Chase even thought that she could see the doctor's reflection in the old-school side mirror.

"It's open," Floyd muttered. "Why's it open?"

Chase shook her head and looked at her fellow FBI Agent.

"What's open?"

Floyd had already entered what appeared to be a processing area of sorts, while Dunbar was holding the outer door open for her.

Chase stepped inside and looked around.

To her right was a glass enclosure, complete with a computer desk and, predictably, an empty chair. In front of her were iron bars.

"The gate."

Floyd's answer wasn't necessary; Chase could see that the inset door in the bars was hanging open by more than a foot.

To her right, Dunbar instinctively put his hand on the butt of his service pistol.

What's he going to shoot? The door?

Chase stepped in front of Floyd and gently pressed the door open.

"M-maybe we should wait here like the d-doctor suggested."

She ignored him and took two steps into the main hallway of the building and then waited for her eyes to adjust to the change in lighting.

There was something on the floor, not twenty feet from where she stood. It was a pile of clothing, old bedding, maybe, or—

"A body!" she shouted, now pulling her own gun free. "It's a fucking body!"

Chapter 22

SLUMPED AGAINST THE WALL was a shirtless man. There was a red butterfly on his chest, but it was hard to discern given the multitude of bloody gashes. His face was covered in white makeup and his lips were painted red with either blood or a vibrant lipstick.

Chase just stared, her mind trying to piece together what had happened here.

Dunbar hurried by her and pressed his fingers to the man's throat. He looked up at Floyd and Chase and shook his head.

The makeup…

"Check for others! Floyd, check for others!" Dunbar instructed as he pulled his walkie out and started to contact headquarters.

…the white powder on my badge after the doctor had taken it.

"Shit!"

Chase headed back through the bars and then into the parking lot, gun held high. The camel-colored car was but a speck on the road leading away from Oak Valley.

Cursing again, Chase ran back into the facility.

Dunbar was still on the radio, while Floyd had started to move down the hallway at a snail's pace, leading with his pistol.

"We need to set up roadblocks!" Chase ordered. "Now!"

In response to her voice, Floyd whipped around, and Chase had to leap out of the way of his gun.

"Floyd! Put the gun down!" Floyd licked his lips nervously and lowered it to his hip. Then, to Dunbar, Chase repeated the order. "We need to get an APB out on the camel-colored car. We need to stop that doctor."

Dunbar nodded.

"One step ahead. I've got my men approaching from all incoming roads."

A dull thump echoed up the hallway, and all three of them fell silent and turned in that direction. When it recurred, Chase once again took charge.

"Floyd, you stay here by the front door. When the NYPD arrives, you make sure you announce who you are and let them know that me and Detective Dunbar are inside. Got it?"

Floyd seemed relieved to not have to go investigate the sound and nodded vigorously.

"And don't fucking shoot anyone."

Chase turned to Dunbar next and indicated with a head nod for them to start down the hallway. Dunbar immediately rose to his feet and took up her left flank. They systematically started to move, clearing rooms on their respective sides in sequence.

The first three were empty, but Chase noticed something in the fourth.

"Dunbar," she said, moving closer to the window.

A figure, clad in all white, was huddled in the corner, their back to her. Chase tapped the glass with the muzzle of her pistol and the figure twitched. Worried that this was another orderly or security guard who had been mauled, she tapped again.

The man in the cell whipped around and then galloped on all fours toward the door. Despite the impenetrable partition separating, the scene was so startling that Chase recoiled, nearly knocking Dunbar over in the process.

There was a dull *thunk* as the man struck the door and then pressed his chest up against it. Laughing maniacally, he then started to lick the glass window in long, wet strokes.

"Jesus."

"You okay?" Dunbar asked.

Chase nodded and shook the visual out of her mind before continuing down the hall.

"Yeah—let's keep moving. Might be more victims."

Dunbar cleared the room on his side of the hall and Chase did the same. Two doors down, Chase came upon a cell that wasn't firmly closed.

"Dunbar," she whispered over her shoulder. Ducking beneath the window, Chase moved to the other side of the door and pressed her back against the wall. Dunbar joined her and pulled the door wide.

"FBI," she exclaimed as she stepped into the room, her gun at hip-level.

When she saw the blood, she immediately called for Dunbar. The detective rushed into the cell, while Chase half-turned to cover their backs.

A moment later, he rose to his feet, the knees of his jeans covered in blood and more of that white makeup.

"Dead," he said in a flat affect.

Chase cursed and then moved back into the hallway.

"Must have been the security guard from the booth—we need to keep moving."

More banging from down the hall spurred their movements. They cleared a few more rooms before Dunbar spoke again.

"I've got something—a woman."

Normally, this wouldn't inspire alarm, but his tone was strange. Chase strode to the opposite side of the hallway and moved in front of Dunbar to peer in through the window.

At long last, it seemed as if they'd found the source of all that banging.

Inside the cell was a pretty woman with short black hair tucked behind her ears. Her face was nearly purple from yelling and pounding on the door. Chase's first thought was that this was just another inmate, but the clothes told a different story: instead of the generic white jumpsuit, she was wearing a t-shirt and jeans.

When the woman finally paused to take a breath and her face returned to a more natural pallor, Chase gasped.

"Shit, I know her. I *know* her." Out of habit, Chase tried to open the door but found it locked. "Just wait—hold on, we'll get you out—"

"Chase?" Another tone shift in Dunbar's voice. This time, he sounded terrified.

"What?" Chase barked, pulling her face away from the glass. "What is it?"

Dunbar didn't say anything this time; he simply pointed at the window of the adjacent cell.

Chase nearly shoved him out of the way and peered inside.

"Oh my god," she moaned, her knees going weak.

Chapter 23

DRAKE WAS SO SHOCKED to see Chase's face fill the window that at first, he didn't even move. But when it looked as if she were about to fall over, he realized how he must have looked to her. Shirtless, blood on his chest and stomach, his gun lying on the ground to his right. With a grunt, he managed to pull himself to his feet. This seemed to rattle Chase even further and somebody, a man, offered her support.

"Dunbar? What the—?" he shook his head. "Chase, get me the fuck out of here!" His throat was raw, his voice hoarse.

Chase's lips moved, but he couldn't hear anything.

"Chase, get me out!" Even though he knew that he should be saving his breath, he couldn't help it. "Let me out!"

Chase just stared, and it took Dunbar pointing down at something that Drake couldn't see to snap her out of it.

There was a metallic scraping sound, and then the slot used to slide a tray and food through suddenly opened.

Fresh air wafted in, and Drake inhaled deeply. He hurried to the door and put his face near the open slot.

"You have to get me out of here. There's a fucking psycho pretending to be a doctor..."

Chase tried to pull the door open, but, of course, it was locked.

She turned to Dunbar.

"Keys? You know where the keys are?"

Dunbar shrugged.

"Never been here before in my life, I'll—"

Drake's eyes suddenly went wide.

"Hanna! Fuck, Hanna's here! Did he get her? Did he—"

"No, she's fine, Drake. Locked up just like you, but fine," Chase replied quickly, and Drake exhaled a sigh of relief.

"What about the tall doctor? Is he—"

"Gone," Chase said with a frown.

"Fuck. Anyone else here?"

Behind Chase, Dunbar was on his radio, hopefully trying to locate a set of keys.

"Two orderlies, both dead—both wearing makeup and butterflies."

Drake groaned and gripped his forehead, realizing that he was wrong. It wasn't Marcus Slasinsky who had killed Mike Brian and he wasn't responsible for kidnapping Louisa or Stitts.

It was Glenn—or whatever the fuck his name was. The question was *why?* What did the butterflies mean to him?

"Drake, you alright? You're bleeding."

Drake looked down at himself and realized that his cut had started to leak again.

"I'm fine. Did you find the damn keys?"

Dunbar moved front and center and shook his head.

"Not yet—my team just arrived, though. Shouldn't be too long before—"

A thought occurred to Drake.

"Ask Hanna—she used to work here. Ask her where they keep the goddamn keys."

Dunbar immediately left the frame and Drake listened as he communicated with Hanna through the flap. And yet, he never took his eyes off Chase.

"I'm sorry, Chase," he said.

Her eyes became slits.

"You lied to me."

"I know, I'm sorry—I thought—"

"You gave him my fucking blood, Drake. My *blood*."

Drake could no longer hold her gaze.

"I'm sorry—" his eyes popped up. "Wait, how did you know that? I didn't—"

Dunbar reappeared and Drake's jaw snapped shut.

"Front office," he informed them. "Hanna said that they keep a set in the front office in a combination locker. I've got a detective in there now. Fair warning, though, the ME is on her way."

Fair warning? Why would—

Drake's heart sunk.

The ME is on her *way. It should be Beckett. God damn it, it should be fucking Beckett.*

"Just hang tight, Drake. We'll have you out in a minute. You and Hanna."

Chapter 24

"ANYTHING?" CHASE ASKED, STEPPING away from the door. She left the tray slot propped open so that Drake could listen.

"Nothing," Dunbar replied. "My men have cordoned off a five-mile radius around Oak Valley, but so far no sighting of either the doctor or his distinctive car."

Chase scowled.

If only I hadn't let him go—I knew *there was something fucked up about the man.*

But it was too late for that now.

Chase looked around and her scowl deepened. There were maybe a dozen cops milling around, a number which would surely double or triple in the coming hours, which would mean that the press would know about it sooner rather than later.

To his credit, Dunbar was doing his best to keep the numbers small, but for every officer he turned away, two more took their place.

Chase wasn't naive, she knew how things in the NYPD worked. The DA could bury a murdered ex-con, keep the media at bay, but now they had three murders on their hands, two of which happened *here*; nothing was more sensationalized than murders at the loony bin.

"Fuck."

She had to act fast. If Marcus Slasinsky got spooked from all this press, her sister was as good as dead.

The problem with that was that the ME had arrived—the same Dr. Nordmeyer that Chase had butted heads with earlier in the day—and she was slow as molasses.

There was also the issue of Hanna and Drake. Dunbar's men had opened the combination locker that was supposed to house the cell keys, but they weren't in there. The fire department had since been called in and even with the jaws of life at their disposal, they were still struggling with the first door: Hanna's.

"Any idea who that guy Glenn was?" Dunbar asked.

"No idea," Chase answered. "Drake?"

"No. Never seen him before."

"Well, Floyd's reviewing the security footage, so hopefully he can find some hints as to the man's identity. I know you wanted to keep this small, Chase, but I've hooked a tech guy up with the detective working the Mike Brian case to try to figure out what all this damn makeup is about."

"Whoever he is, he's working with Marcus, which means that if we find Glenn, we find the others."

"Wait—how do you know that?" Drake asked from inside his cell. "Glenn could be a copycat or a fucking bug nut for all we know."

Dunbar shot Chase a look, a silent indication that she could reveal as little or as much as she wanted to.

Chase, however, was done keeping secrets. Despite Drake's actions, the fact that he'd come here even before she had the idea, was a clear indication that she needed him on her side.

Still, the sheer audacity of what he'd done, and the accompanying deep-rooted feeling of violation, remained front and center.

"They tested the blood that they found on Mike Brian's chest and it came back as mine," Chase said. "Which leaves one of two possibilities: either Marcus is behind this or he sold my blood to a like-minded psychopath. And, given what you've told me already, Drake, I doubt any price would be high enough for the man to sell his precious spank bank material."

Dunbar shifted uncomfortably as Chase's words hung in the air.

Eventually, Drake spoke up.

"That doesn't make sense, if—"

There was a loud pop followed by crunching metal and the two firefighters suddenly stepped away from the door to Hanna's cell.

"It's open," one of them said, as if this wasn't obvious. Hanna appeared almost instantly, hands on her knees, breathing deeply.

She appeared not only winded but also terrified.

"Somebody get a paramedic over here," the other firefighter hollered. "Let's give her a—"

Hanna waved her hand dismissively.

"I'm fine. Just get Drake out."

Chase had met the woman several times under similarly tense circumstances. She briefly wondered why Drake was so close with her, given Hanna's checkered past, before shaking free of these feelings.

Pot and Kettle and all that.

Hanna was taller than Chase, but only by a few inches. And while the PI's hair was a slightly lighter shade, it was about the same length as hers. They were also both small in stature and had pretty faces.

"When did you guys come here?"

"Not sure—an hour ago, maybe two. Thought I could call in some favors from people I know here and get a look at the security footage of when Marcus was here. That asshole Glenn tricked us."

Just talking about what had happened was enough to cause Hanna to breathe more rapidly, but this time Chase couldn't tell if it was because she was scared or just angry.

Probably a bit of both.

"Did you know him?" Chase asked. "Glenn, I mean?"

Hanna nodded.

"No. He said he was new, but... *fuck*."

Having since figured out how Hanna's door worked, the firefighters were much more efficient with Drake's. Within moments he was freed.

"Let me guess, you don't want a paramedic, either," the same firefighter who had asked Hanna said.

"No. Just a new shirt would be nice."

Someone handed him one and he slipped it on. Forgoing any sort of formalities, Drake jumped right into the conversation.

"If what you say about the blood is true, Chase, then I'm pretty sure Marcus set us up, that he knew as soon as we figured out he was involved, that we'd come here." Drake snapped his fingers. "And that Glenn guy? He wasn't a doctor... he was a *patient*."

Chase made a face.

"A patient?"

Drake nodded.

"Yeah, he said something strange to me before we were ambushed... he said that it's not as busy in Oak Valley as when I was here." He turned to Dunbar. "Check the patient records for a Glenn something. If they have intake pictures, review those as well; someone as tall and weird looking as him is hard to miss."

Hanna suddenly cursed. Apparently, she recognized the murdered orderly in the hallway.

Chase looked at her, then Drake, then the corpse.

Why... why didn't he kill Drake and Hanna? Why let them live? Why lock them up?

"Chase?" Drake asked in a concerned tone.

For some reason, Chase couldn't look away from Hanna.

"Yeah, he acted weird with me, too. I showed him my badge outside, and he looked at it for a long time like he didn't believe that it was really me. It was like—" All four chambers of Chase's heart seemed to contract at once.

"What's wrong?"

Chase turned to Dunbar.

"You need to get everyone out of here, Dunbar."

"What? What are you talking about?"

"You need to get all of the cops out of here, *now!*"

Chapter 25

THE INSTANT THE WORDS came out of Chase's mouth, Drake knew that she was right.

This whole thing had been a setup. Drake had had an inkling while sitting in his cell staring at his knife wound, but now he was sure of it: it was all connected. Marcus knew that as soon as the blood on Mike Brian's corpse was entered into NDIS, the FBI would be notified, and Chase would find out.

Marcus also knew that when they discovered that he was involved they would come here, to Oak Valley.

The only part that Drake hadn't deduced on his own, was that Psycho Glenn had made a mistake: he must have thought that Hanna was Chase and that was why he'd thrown them both into their respective cells.

Marcus Slasinsky had obviously instructed the man not to harm them, just to keep them here instead until he showed up to… well, finish what he'd started all those years ago.

"Dunbar, let's get your men moving! We can't let Marcus know you're here," Chase implored.

But even with Dunbar and Chase barking orders, the confused police officers were taking their sweet ass time. It didn't help that Dr. Nordmeyer was performing the most ridiculously intricate examinations of the corpses as if there was still a slim hope of revival.

"Move!"

Dunbar took out his walkie.

"Pull the roadblocks," he instructed. "Keep the APB for the brown car, but don't stop vehicles coming in or out. I want a perimeter around the building but stay out of sight. I don't want a single officer visible."

A uniformed officer leaned over and whispered something into Dunbar's ear. Dunbar nodded and then brought his walkie to his mouth once more.

"We have three patients inside, but no staff. I want Richards and Oppenheim to grab an orderly uniform and slip it on. But I don't want either of you to be seen. Got it?"

Drake watched the commotion with abject confusion. It had been a long time since he'd worked with others, and longer still since he wasn't the one in charge.

He wasn't sure he liked it.

Chase passed right by him without a word and made her way to Dr. Nordmeyer, who was crouched over the corpse in the hallway.

The woman looked up at her as she approached and preemptively said, "I need to take samples from—"

Chase shook her head.

"Do it at the lab."

Dr. Nordmeyer looked as if she were about to protest, but the expression on Chase's face convinced her otherwise. She immediately started packing up her tools.

"If anything happens to this body, or if the scene is compromised—"

"Yeah, yeah, my responsibility, I get it. Now get the hell out of here."

It took another five minutes before everyone cleared out, except for undercover Officers Richards and Oppenheim who were hidden out of sight. When it was just the four of them—Dunbar, Drake, Chase, and Hanna—Chase began laying out her plan.

"Hanna, you come with me—we'll be parked outside waiting for Marcus to show. Dunbar, you be at the ready with your men, relay with Richards and Oppenheim, if we need them." She paused to take a breath.

"What about me?" Drake asked.

Chase frowned.

"Go meet Floyd in the security room, review the tapes," she said flatly.

Now it was Drake's turn to grimace.

"What? No, I need to—"

Chase suddenly turned to him.

"Don't you think you've done enough? Huh?"

Drake's eyebrows lifted and he glanced at Dunbar then Hanna, both of whom looked incredibly uncomfortable.

"Chase, I said I was—"

"We don't have time for that now. Go meet Floyd."

The last thing Drake wanted to do was be staring at a computer screen right now. He needed to be by Chase's side when this all went down.

"You want Drake on a computer?" Hanna said, a wry grin on her face. "He can't even text with those sausage fingers. *I'll* help Floyd—besides, I don't have my gun with me, but Drake does. He should go with you."

Chase's jaw clenched, but before she could object, Dunbar chimed in.

"Yeah, that's a better idea—safer. Now let's get just the fuck out of sight."

Without waiting for a reply, Dunbar turned and started down the hallway, making a wide berth around the painted corpse.

"Fuck," Chase grumbled. "Alright, you're with me, Drake, but only until Marcus gets here. After that, you're on your own."

Chapter 26

THE LONGER THAT DRAKE and Chase sat in her BMW in silence, the less likely it was that Marcus would show. Their only hope was that either they had spooked Glenn so badly that he forgot to notify the man of his fuck up, or that he was scared of the repercussions as a result of mistaking Hanna for Chase.

Chase kept waiting for Drake to speak as they waited, but despite his recent changes, the man still didn't appear to be big on words. And as much as she wanted Dunbar or Floyd or anyone to be in the car with her instead of Drake, she could only handle so much silence before her thoughts started to turn dark.

"Where did you get my blood from, anyway? Did you steal from me when I was a sergeant?"

Drake kept his eyes trained on the small road between them and Oak Valley.

"I'd rather not say."

Chase frowned.

More secrets—great.

"That's fucked up, Drake."

Drake took a deep breath and turned to look at her.

"I know—I know it's fucked up. This whole thing is fucked up. Me being back here in New York City? That's fucked up. Me being in a car with you like when we were both in the NYPD? That's fucked up. Marcus Slasinsky on the loose? That's fucked up."

"I saw him, you know. Or at least I think I did."

Drake's eyes narrowed.

"What do you mean?"

Chase looked away. She wasn't sure if she should tell Drake about her sister, but if she really thought that he could help, what choice did she have?

"I saw a video of Stitts being led from the bar by the man—by Marcus—and my..." she swallowed hard. "...my sister."

"*What?* Your sister? I thought—"

"I found her, Drake. After all these years, I found her."

After a short pause, Chase laid it all out on the table. She told Drake about finding her sister, about rescuing her from the clutches of two demented brothers and how she'd killed one of them. Chase even went as far as to tell him what she'd never told anyone before, not even Stitts: that her sister was angry with her, furious, even, and that she'd vowed revenge.

"Chase, I'm sorry. That's..."

"Fucked up," she finished for him. "And now Marcus has her, too—she was on that video from the bar. She's under his spell, Drake. We both know how manipulative he can be..." Chase let her sentence trail off, hoping that Drake would chime in.

But when the man didn't speak for several moments, a familiar, uncomfortable itching sensation rolled up and down her forearms.

Say something... anything. Please.

Chase was aware of how Floyd and Dunbar felt about her theory regarding Georgina's involvement in all of this, but that was only because they didn't know Dr. Mark Kruk, didn't know him the way they did.

"Drake?"

"I... I know how complicated family can be, Chase," he said in a strange voice. "I just want to help you find her—find *them*.

I'm sorry about this whole thing, about feeding Marcus' obsession. But I only did it because I *had* to. I get that it's not fair, I do, but I was hoping that you would understand."

"I didn't ask for any of this," Chase shot back.

Anger was easier than compassion, and it floated to the surface of even the most stagnant of swamps.

"I know you didn't, and again, I apologize. Of all people, though, I thought you would understand."

Chase glared at him now, but he refused to meet her gaze.

You thought I would understand? You thought I would be okay with you giving my blood to an obsessed serial killer?

And yet, even as these thoughts formulated in her mind, Chase was considering her own actions. During her tenure in the FBI, she'd done a great many things that others had frowned upon. Shit, most of them would have cost anybody else their job, and several should have landed her in prison.

Instead, Chase was here, given any and all of the resources at the FBI's disposal to find her sister and her friends.

Sometimes the route to good outcomes was an arduous one consisting of switchback roads peppered with potholes and dangerous cliffs.

Chase stood at a fork now; one way meant harboring anger towards Drake, the other meant forgiveness. Chase stood in the middle for some time, unsure of which way led to the top of the mountain.

In the end, she decided that no matter which route she chose, moving forward was the only option.

Her eyes drifted from Drake's face to the psychiatric facility looming in front of them.

"You really stayed here?"

Drake nodded.

"Yep."

"How was it? I mean, being locked up in a cell like that?"

Chase was thinking about her own demons, and how she only knew of three ways of silencing them: throwing herself into her work, sleeping with shady characters, or numbing herself with illicit substances.

"I'll tell you this, Chase: if you're not crazy when you go in there, there's a high probability that you will be when you come out."

Chase's first thought was that Drake was making a joke. His stone-cold expression suggested otherwise.

"If I went in there, I doubt I'd ever come out again," she said quietly. After clearing her throat, Chase added, "One day, when this is all over, we'll sit down, get drunk, and just let it all hang out."

"Yeah, it's just too bad Beckett won't be around to join us."

Chase's shoulders slumped and she sunk into her leather seat.

Giving Marcus her blood was something they could work out. Shit, even her sister's twisted logic could be overcome, given enough time.

But Beckett's death was permanent.

"I'm sorry about—"

"Shh," Drake suddenly hushed her. "Look."

A black car was rolling down the road in front of them. At first, it looked as if it was just going to drive on by, but it slowed and eventually stopped by the entrance to the parking lot. After a few seconds, the four-way flashers came on.

"What the hell?" Chase muttered under breath. She grabbed the walkie that Dunbar had given her off the dashboard. "There's a car stopped out front."

"Want us to come out?" Dunbar replied nearly instantly.

"No, Drake and I will investigate. Just be ready."

Chase looked over at Drake and wasn't surprised that he had his gun in his hand and was already reaching for the door handle.

She could question his actions, his decisions, and maybe even his motivation, but the one thing that was never in doubt was Drake's loyalty.

"You ready?" he asked.

Chase shook her head, but she was already stepping out of the car.

She wasn't ready; she wasn't ready to see her sister again after what had happened the last time.

And maybe she never would be.

But that didn't change the fact that Chase had a job to do, and friends to save.

"I'm ready," she said, pulling her gun from the holster. "Let's do this."

Chapter 27

DRAKE APPROACHED FROM THE front, and Chase from the rear. The windows were so heavily tinted, that neither could see inside the vehicle.

"Turn off the car," Drake ordered, training his gun at where the driver would be sitting. The engine turned off, but the flashers remained on.

"Open the window."

As the window started to roll down, Drake adjusted his grip on the gun and slid toward the driver side door.

"Drop the keys out the window and then open the door from the outside."

Again, the driver, who was shrouded in shadows, did as they were asked. Drake could tell by the hands that the driver was a young male, but a dark sweatshirt with a hoodie pulled over his head hid any other discernible features.

"Now step out of the—"

Chase suddenly rushed at the man. This caught Drake by surprise and before he could even react, she had grabbed the back of his hoodie and wrenched it off so hard that the man was yanked fully out of the car.

"Please," the man pleaded, his hands going into the air. "Please, don't hurt me."

It wasn't Marcus Slasinsky.

Drake straddled the man while Chase took a step back.

"Who are you?"

Before he could answer, Chase followed this up with another question.

"Where are *they*?"

The young man, who had a narrow face and dark, greasy hair, looked from Drake to Chase and back again, confusion coming in waves.

"Where the fuck are *they*?" Chase screamed.

"What? I don't—what are you talking about? *Wh-who* are you talking about?"

"Chase, check the back seat."

But either Chase didn't hear Drake, or she ignored him. Her face red with anger, she moved forward again and leveled the gun at the man's chest.

"Ah, fuck, Jesus, please, don't hurt me!" the man closed his eyes and started to shake. "I just came—ah—I just came to deliver a package. Please don't hurt me."

"What package?"

The man's eyes opened wide and he stared at Drake.

"A box—just a box. Please…"

Chase's jaw clenched and for a fleeting moment, Drake thought that she had lost it completely and was going to shoot the poor kid.

"Chase—"

She whipped around, her gun still clutched in her hand.

"Jesus, put the fucking gun down, Chase!"

Chase didn't listen, but Drake was relieved to see that her finger had slipped from the trigger to the guard.

"Where are they?" she demanded, turning back to the cowering man.

"I don't have no fucking clue what you're talking about! I just got five hundred bucks to deliver a package here. That's it. Please, just don't fucking shoot me."

Drake swore under his breath.

This wasn't Marcus Slasinsky, Georgina Adams, Jeremy Stitts, or Louisa Palmer. This was a nobody—just another cog in Marcus' fucked up plan to mess with them.

Chase must have realized this too because she finally lowered the gun and reached for her walkie.

"Dunbar, get your ass out here." Then to the man slumped on the ground in front of his car, she said, "What package?"

But he was so frightened that he couldn't even manage a single word now.

"What package?" Chase screamed.

The man started to sob, and Drake saw the front of his jeans go dark.

"Puh-puh-please don't kill me," he blubbered. "Puh-puh-please."

"She's not going to kill you—she's FBI," Drake said, but despite his words, he wasn't a hundred percent sure. Chase looked like she was hanging on by a thread.

"Go check the trunk," he said quickly. "Chase, go check the trunk."

Chase scowled at him but eventually grabbed the keys from where they lay in the dirt and made her way around the back of the car.

"You're going to tell me exactly where you got this package from and who gave it to you."

The man wiped the snot from his face with the back of his arm and then nodded vigorously.

"I-I-I was in a bar downtown—*B-Barney's*—and some guy just came in, said he needed a p-p-package delivered. Was gonna pay five hundred b-b-b-bucks, upfront. I thought—I mean, I looked, and it wasn't drugs or a bomb or nothing, just a stupid fucking dress and I mean, how c-c-could I—"

A dress?

Drake shook his head and tried to remain focused.

"Who gave you the box?"

"I never seen him before—I swear. Didn't give me a name or nothing. Fuck man, I—"

"And he told you to come here? To *this* place?"

In his periphery, he saw Chase open the trunk.

"Yeah, right here, fuck. I didn't even know—" he started to turn his head.

"Look at me!"

The man's wet eyes returned to front and center.

"—I just had an address, m-man. Please, you gotta let me go. I didn't mean to do nothing wrong."

Floyd and Hanna were making their way toward the car from the building now, while Dunbar was fast approaching on foot from their left.

"You had no idea that this was—"

Chase gasped and Drake looked over at her. She was slowly moving away from the trunk, her face pale. Keeping his gun locked on the man on the ground, he made his way toward her.

"What is it? Chase? What's in the trunk?"

When she didn't answer right away, he finally took his eyes off the delivery man and looked inside.

Lying in the center of the trunk was a plain brown box. The top flaps hung open, revealing what looked to Drake like some sort of old-fashioned, off-white tablecloth.

"What the hell is that?" he asked.

"It's her dress," Chase replied.

"Her *dress*?" Drake shook his head. "*Whose* dress? Chase, what the fuck is going on?"

Chase staggered.

"Georgina's... that's my sister's dress, Drake. I told you Marcus has her. I fucking *told* you."

Chapter 28

CHASE TRIED TO BACKPEDAL, but her legs and feet refused to respond. The only reason she didn't go down was because Drake held her up.

"Breathe, Chase, Breathe."

Hanna seemed unconcerned by her condition and went directly to the trunk and pulled the box out. She set it on the ground and was about to reach inside when Dunbar appeared.

"Don't touch it," the detective warned. Hanna made a face, and Dunbar clarified. "I want to see if I can pull some prints off it."

Hanna continued to stare, making it clear that this was unnecessary: they already knew who had sent the box.

"Maybe you should sit down," Drake suggested.

Chase did the opposite; she straightened and pulled out of his grasp.

"I'll be fine." As if to prove this point, she looked around, scanning the road in either direction. "He's not coming—Marcus isn't coming."

"Maybe we should just wait a little while longer," Dunbar said. "Just to be sure."

Chase shook her head.

"He's been one step ahead of us the whole time—he's stringing us along, and he's using my sister to do it."

"Hey, you," Drake said, raising his voice for the whimpering man on the ground to hear. "When did you pick up the package?"

"L-last night."

Drake nodded.

"Yeah, Marcus knew alright; he knew that we'd find the body and knew that we would come here. He probably guessed that either Glenn would fuck up or that we wouldn't fall for it—he planned this delivery even before Glenn took off and could have told him what happened."

The five of them all stood in a small circle, staring at the ground.

Except for Chase; she was staring at the dress, recalling how Georgina and all of her sisters were wearing the exact same thing when they'd found them.

How she'd tried one just like it on, herself.

"Alright, I'm shutting this thing down," Dunbar said, finally breaking the silence. "I'll get CSU to come in and some staff to look after the remaining inmates."

"Yeah, and how about some fucking security? When I was here, it was like Rikers Island. Now it seems that everyone can just come and go as they please."

Chase shot him a look, and Drake, clearly not realizing what he was saying, grumbled something apologetic.

"What about him?" Hanna asked, raising her chin to the delivery man.

Dunbar cocked his head.

"I'll bring him in, press him a little."

The tone of the detective's voice was telling; he didn't believe that anything would come of this, and neither did Chase. Still, they couldn't just let him walk.

"I'll also take the box and dress for processing and—"

"I want it," Chase blurted.

All eyes were suddenly on her.

"I want the dress."

Drake reached out with a comforting hand, but she moved beyond his grasp.

"Chase, it's evidence. You—"

"I want it," she repeated for a third time.

Eventually, Dunbar shrugged.

"It's your investigation, Chase. I just don't want to be responsible if there are problems getting things entered into evidence for a trial."

Chase reached down and picked up the dress. The fabric was coarse, but she rubbed it against her palm nonetheless.

Somehow, she managed to resist the urge to smell it, to smell her sister. Even so, Chase knew instantly that this was *her* dress and not one of the others' or an imitation.

Trial? This thing isn't going to trial. No fucking way is it going to trial.

"Well, that was a bit of a lunch bag let down," Hanna said with a grimace. "But not all is lost."

"What do you mean?" Drake asked.

"Floyd and I found something on the tapes—something I think all of you are going to want to see."

Chapter 29

"YEAH, I'LL CATCH UP," Drake said as Hanna, Chase, and Floyd started back toward Oak Valley.

Drake watched them go, and then helped Dunbar cuff the man and put him in the back of his police car, which one of the officers had been kind enough to pull around for him. Then he took the man aside.

"Chase's sister isn't a victim here, is she?"

Dunbar seemed surprised by the question, but his answer was as expected.

"No—not in the least. But Chase won't listen to us, she's already made up her mind."

Drake nodded. He'd suspected as much when Chase had first told him of Georgina's involvement in her BMW. Rarely one to explain herself, Chase had all but bent over backward trying to convince him that Georgina was a victim.

"Fuck, that's what I thought. Alright, well, it doesn't matter now—hopefully, it won't matter later, either. What about keeping the press in the dark? You think that's the right idea?"

Dunbar chewed the inside of his cheek before answering.

"I don't—think it's a bad idea. The DA wants to push everything under the rug, including Marcus' escape. I think we should blow it up, put some pressure on him and everyone. Besides, we have three dead bodies now, Drake, three dead bodies with butterflies and fucking makeup."

Drake agreed, but for a different reason.

"Marcus has been predicting everything that we've done so far… let me ask you something, this video? The one that shows Chase's sister? Did you get a good look at her face?"

"She stared right into the camera."

"Yeah, that's what I thought. Marcus probably made sure of it, because he knew that once Chase saw the video—which he was certain would happen—that she would refuse to make it public to protect Georgina."

Dunbar scratched the back of his neck.

"What do we do, Drake?"

"Stay the course, for now, anyway. But I think that there's going to be a point when we have to push this out to the media—*hard*." Drake paused. "In spite of what Chase might say."

"It's her case, Drake," Dunbar reminded him.

"Yeah? And since when did that matter?"

Dunbar shifted uncomfortably.

"Since I vouched for you, since Chase got you a day pass."

Drake's eyes narrowed.

"Yeah, she got me out to help her—she didn't get me out so that I could just be her lackey. If that were the case, she could just get any number of your men who keep eye-raping her to help out."

"Drake, I know what you've been through. I know what happened to you in prison and—"

"Doesn't matter. The only thing that matters is finding Stitts and Louisa before Marcus kills them. When this is over, I'm fully prepared to go back behind bars, so you don't need to worry about that."

"That's not what I meant."

Drake shook his head.

"We're wasting time here. I just want to make sure that if it comes down to it, we're going to do whatever we have to to get these people back."

No matter what Chase says, Drake implied but didn't say.

Dunbar appeared to catch his drift, but before he could answer, a young police officer suddenly bounded around the car and approached them.

"Detective Dunbar?"

"Yeah?"

"Got a news van at the end of the road, wants a statement. What do you want me to do?"

Dunbar looked to Drake, who shook his head.

Not yet. Soon, but not yet.

"Tell them nothing," Dunbar replied, his face expressionless. "Make sure that the other officers keep their mouths shut."

"Got it." The man turned to leave but noticed Drake at the last moment and stopped. "Hey, aren't you—aren't you—"

"The Easter Bunny."

"Go on," Dunbar instructed. "Keep the press out."

The officer frowned but hurried off without another word. Drake headed in the other direction, toward Oak Valley.

"Hey, where are you going?" Dunbar hollered.

"To figure out how to stop Marcus from killing people," Drake shot back.

And to make sure that Chase doesn't lose her mind.

Chapter 30

Drake knew that he should be surprised, but he wasn't. After all, Glenn had told him when they'd first arrived, in not so many words, that he had been there before.

Glenn Brick had been a patient at Oak Valley Psychiatric Facility—*was* still a patient, technically speaking.

"Found this footage from about two weeks ago," Hanna said, drawing their attention to the monitor. It was a video taken from the front entrance, showing a man in a doctor's coat entering the facility. He had dark hair and glasses, and there was a folder in his hands. He walked directly up to the glass booth where Hanna had once worked and started to converse with her replacement. After a few moments of what appeared to be idle chit-chat—there was no audio—the man slid a sheet of paper and what appeared to be an ID card in the slot.

With his head still down, avoiding showing his face directly to the camera, the man tapped his foot and waited. A minute later, the bars opened, and his credentials were passed back to him.

If that had been the end of the video, Drake would've thought nothing of it; to him, it appeared like everything was normal.

But as the figure in the white coat started to make his way through the iron bars and into the hallway, he turned back and looked up at the camera.

It appeared as if Hanna wasn't the only one with the innate ability to be a chameleon.

It had been about six months since Drake had seen the man's face, but it wasn't one that he would easily forget: the man in the white coat was Marcus Slasinsky—the Butterfly Killer—or, more fitting in this environment, Dr. Mark Kruk, the persona he'd adopted after suffering severe PTSD as a child.

It was the man whom Drake had spoken with in this very facility when they'd both been patients.

"That's him," Chase whispered under her breath.

Her body was trembling slightly, and Drake realized that she was still reeling from seeing her sister's dress. At least she didn't seem to have it on her anymore, which Drake supposed was something positive.

A small step toward letting go.

"Oh, that's him all right," Hanna muttered.

Drake realized that there was a hint of guilt in her voice, which, in turn, triggered guilt in himself. After all, if it hadn't been for him, Hanna never would have gotten herself involved with Marcus Slasinsky's or his subsequent escape.

"Now watch this from less than an hour later."

Hanna booted up a new video and they were once again staring at the entrance to the facility. Only this time, the bars opened first, and Marcus Slasinsky stepped into view. He said something to the woman behind the desk and then pulled a much taller man with rolled shoulders and his chin pressed to his chest into view.

More paperwork, then the front door opened, and the two men started out. But just before leaving the frame, Marcus yanked on the handcuffs that bound his prisoner's wrists and the man looked up, a pained expression on his oddly smooth face.

"And that's Glenn Brick," Hanna informed them.

Drake felt his upper lip curl.

It was the same man who had let both him and Hanna into Oak Valley only to accost him with a knife and shove them into adjacent cells.

"How is this possible?" Chase demanded. "What the hell kind of backwoods security does this place have?"

"I'm guessing that things were a little h-hectic, what with the DA wanting to move prisoners to other facilities after Marcus' escape," Floyd offered. "To t-try to get the public off his back."

Yeah, but even before that, all you needed was to know the right people, and you could *get out,* Drake thought. *Maybe everyone would have been better off if Hanna had just said no when I asked her to help me out.*

"What a joke. But he did have paperwork—I saw that asshole hand something over."

"Yep—it's right there, right beside Glenn's psych eval," Hanna told them.

Chase quickly picked up a stack of admission and discharge orders and started to scan through them. Drake read over her shoulder and stopped her when he saw a single sheet of paper with a date that matched the video time code.

"Right there," he said, pointing at a specific line. "Looks like Glenn Brick was signed out by... Dr. Matteo? Who the hell is that?"

Hanna shrugged and they all turned to Chase for an answer. She didn't say anything, but her trembling increased, and the piece of paper started to make a funny waffling sound.

"And there—the discharge order was approved by... Christopher Hampton?" Drake shook his head. "Who the fuck are these people?"

"Wait? Did you say Chris *Hampton*?" Floyd asked, pulling away from the computer.

"Yeah. Right there. Christopher—"

"They're my people," Chase said under her breath. She swung around in the chair to look at Drake. "Dr. Matteo is my psychiatrist and Christopher Hampton is the Director of the FBI at Quantico."

Drake's eyes bulged.

"*What*? Why would they—"

Before he could finish the sentence, Hanna spoke up.

"They didn't—there's no fucking way they signed off on this. Whoever my replacement is was too busy doing her nails and checking Instagram to actually follow-up on this. I'm guessing that Marcus Slasinsky knew how lax security could be from when he was a patient…" she paused. "When *we* were here."

Drake cursed under his breath.

"What balls on this bastard. He escapes from the facility and then comes back pretending to be someone else only to help another inmate escape."

Chase ignored the comment.

"It's me he wants," she said softly. "He doesn't want Stitts, he doesn't want Louisa, and he doesn't want Georgina. It's me. All of this is about me. I'm the one he wants."

An awkward pause fell over the room.

"Chase, I think—"

Chase suddenly rose to her feet.

"Well, you prick, if you want me, I'm right here. What the hell are you waiting for?"

Chapter 31

"CHASE? CHASE, WHERE ARE you going?" Drake hollered as he stepped into the hallway. "Chase?"

The woman didn't even stop walking, let alone turn.

"Wh-what should we do now?"

Drake poked his head back into the security room. It felt odd being asked for direction, given the fact that he was perhaps the one with the least amount of authority here. Still, he had experience on his side, and it looked like both Floyd and Hanna were at a loss for what to do next.

"Shit," Drake scratched his beard. "That asshole who dropped off the dress said something about being hired by a random at Barney's. Floyd, why don't you head out there, see if there's any video. Let him know that you're a friend of mine and he should be able to help you out."

Floyd nodded and then quickly started to pack up his things.

"What about me?" Hanna asked.

Drake looked around.

"You're more familiar with this place than anyone. Keep on digging into the footage of Marcus and Glenn, look around, see if you can figure out what the hell they were talking about."

Hanna gave him a mock salute.

"What about you?"

Drake leaned into the hallway and frowned when he saw that Chase was already gone.

"I'm going with her, I guess," he said under his breath.

***

Drake found Chase in the parking lot, rooting through her trunk.

"Chase?"

He turned the corner just in time to see Chase shoving the white dress back into the trunk before slamming it closed.

"What?"

"What do you mean, 'what'? I'm here to fucking help, Chase—but I can't do that if you keep on running off."

Chase brushed by him and opened the door to her BMW.

"Yeah, well, it's me he wants, not you."

"For fuck's—" Drake realized that the police had since returned to Oak Valley and that there were many sets of eyes on them. He lowered his voice. "Yeah, I know. Trust me, I know—I was there all those years ago, remember? But here's the thing: Marcus has been playing with us, toying with us. He's pulling the goddamn strings here. I'm thinking that you going after him alone is exactly what he wants."

This seemed to strike a nerve with Chase as she stopped halfway into her car and turned to look at him.

As self-confident and determined as she was, it was clear by her expression that she, like Floyd and Hanna back in the facility, was looking for some direction.

"Yeah?"

"Yeah."

It appeared as if the idea of playing into Marcus' hands was so abhorrent that it overcame Chase's stubborn streak. For now, anyway.

"So, what am I supposed to do, Drake? Just stop looking for him?"

"No, I think—" Drake paused. "You know what? That's actually a good idea."

Chase shook her head and got into her car.

"Too many daiquiris and too much sun has scrambled your brains, Drake."

With that, she closed the door and started the car. This time, however, Drake wasn't letting her get off that easily. He hurried to the passenger side and got in without waiting for an invitation.

Chase put the car into drive but didn't go anywhere. After staring straight ahead for a good ten-count, she shifted the BMW into park and looked at him.

"Well, what do you suggest that I do, then? And if you say, sit around and wait, I'll—"

Drake shook his head.

"Hell no. But instead of going after Marcus like he expects, let's go after someone else instead."

Chase stared at him but eventually started to nod.

"Glenn."

"Yep."

She put the car into drive again, but this time started out of the parking lot.

"Where are we going?" Drake asked.

"If Glenn Brick was sentenced to Oak Valley, the same place you were shipped off to, I'm betting that he was booked at 62nd precinct. What do you think?"

Drake scowled and turned his gaze out the window.

"I think that's pretty much the last place on earth that I want to go today... or ever again."

Chapter 32

"HEY, YOU'RE ONE OF Drake's friends, aren't you?"

The bartender asked the second that Floyd stepped through the doors.

"S-something like that," he replied.

"Well, you're a cop, anyway. What can I do for you?"

The place was nearly empty, which was a good sign. In Floyd's limited experience, bartenders and proprietors didn't really like to have brass in their establishments for an extended period of time. Just wasn't good for business.

"Actually, I'm FBI," Floyd said, quickly flashing his badge.

The man behind the bar spread his mustache with the thumb and forefinger of one hand.

"I'd stick to being Drake's friend… that'll get you further around here."

"Uh, y-yeah."

"Alright, man, what can I do for you? For Drake? And what do you want to drink?"

Floyd leaned in close.

"No, no drink for me, thanks. As for what you can do for me… you wouldn't happen to have any security cameras in here, would you?"

***

"Everything's in here," Mickey said as he opened the door to a storage room at the end of a long, dark hallway. "The tapes are all digital, so you can just search by date."

Floyd was only half-listening; the moment the door opened, he took up residence in the dusty armchair and woke up the computer. He was surprised to see that there was no username or password necessary.

"You looking for when Drake was here last? I mean, before the other day? Gotta be six or seven months ago."

Floyd's fingers stopped dancing across the keyboard.

"You keep video for that long?" he asked.

"Yeah, sometimes... you never know when it might come in handy. I think the system starts to override old files after a month or two, but I sometimes flag ones of interest."

The answer seemed odd—*why would Mickey, Drake's friend, keep videos of him?*— but Floyd let it go. He wasn't here to question the man's judgment or security footage maintenance strategies.

As he started to review videos from last night as per the delivery man's claims, Mickey hung out in the doorway. This made Floyd uncomfortable—decades of living with a stutter had rendered him self-conscious about nearly everything—but it wasn't as if he could ask the man to leave. It was his bar, after all, and he had no obligation whatsoever to allow Floyd access to his security footage.

If Chase were here, however, Floyd had no doubt that she would have told the mustachioed bartender to buzz off.

The man would listen, too, because... well, because it was Chase.

Floyd tried to concentrate as he sped up the footage to one and a half times speed, but his mind just kept coming back to the other video he'd seen today.

The one that showed Marcus and Georgina carrying Stitts away from the bar. No matter how convinced Chase was that her sister was a victim, Floyd knew differently.

He'd seen the look in Georgina Adams' face. She wasn't a poor, lost or manipulated soul at the mercy of a psychopath with deep insight into the human mind.

No, she was a willing participant, someone who knew exactly what they were doing.

The only thing that Floyd didn't understand was the *why*.

He'd reviewed Stitts' and Chase's report about the incident in Tennessee at Director Hampton's behest after showing the man the video, even though it had made him feel... *dishonest*.

Chase had saved her sister not only from her captors—one of whom ended up dead by Chase's hand—but had also managed to somehow shield Georgina from the scrutiny that the other victims were subjected to following the raid.

Curious, Floyd had even placed a call into the Tennessee Bureau of Investigation, but the man he'd been forwarded to, Terrence Conway, had been less than forthcoming with the information.

On-screen, a man in a black outfit walked into the bar, holding a box in his hands.

Floyd immediately slowed the video to real-time and watched in earnest. The man was holding the box in one hand and saying something to anyone who would listen. It was clear by his actions that he was trying to get someone to take the box off his hands.

But, drunk or not, most of Barney's patrons ignored the stranger.

That is, until a man who had been sitting at the back of the bar sipping beer for the better part of two hours, suddenly stood and stepped forward.

"Bingo," Floyd whispered. The two men struck up a conversation and eventually the man with the box put it on the table. The second man, the one that Floyd recognized as the delivery man, looked inside, nodded, and then took an envelope from the man in the dark outfit.

Floyd went forward and backward on the video until he managed to get a fairly clear shot of the face of the man who had brought the box into Barney's. He had a large nose, eyes that were close together, and a gap between his two front teeth. It was dark in the bar, but if Floyd had to guess, he would peg the man as being either of Filipino or Thai descent.

"Find something interesting?" Mickey asked.

"Yeah, I think I did. Do you—do you recognize this man?"

Mickey unfolded his arms from his chest and moved from the doorway to behind Floyd's chair.

"Huh—yeah, I know him. His name is Randy Kong. He's a regular, has been for years."

Floyd was pleasantly surprised.

"Really?"

"Yeah. As I said, he's a regular."

Floyd stared into Randy Kong's eyes as if he could see into his mind and figure out how he was connected to Marcus Slasinsky and Glenn Brick.

"Do you remember him from last night? Came in with a cardboard box?"

Mickey made a face.

"Naw—was off last night. I can ask my—"

"No, no, that's fine. Do me a favor and make sure that this video doesn't get deleted?" Floyd asked, rising to his feet. He took out his cell phone and snapped a picture of Randy Kong.

"Yeah, no problem. Anything else I can do for you?"

Floyd started to shake his head, but then stopped.

"You know what? Think I can have a few more minutes with this thing?"

Mickey nodded.

"Sure. But I'm going to have to head back to the bar."

"Y-yeah, no problem. One more thing: you said Drake was last here six months ago, is that right?"

Chapter 33

"I CAN'T GO IN there," Drake said as he stared up at 62nd precinct.

Chase nodded. She knew by the look on his face that it wasn't just because of the feelings the other NYPD officers harbored for him, but the fact that he'd actually been a prisoner here not that long ago.

Drake had already been locked in a cell that he'd previously occupied once today back at Oak Valley and it was clear that he didn't want to risk that happening again.

"I'll go," she said. "You stay put."

Before he could protest, Chase got out of the car and strode toward the front doors, ignoring stares from officers that were milling about the parking lot.

Drake's idea of coming after Glenn had some merit—and she loathed the idea of following the breadcrumbs that Marcus had left for her—but if this didn't pan out, she wouldn't hesitate to hunt the Butterfly Killer again.

The longer she spent here, the greater the chance that Marcus would send her another package. Only this time, she had a feeling that it wouldn't be an article of clothing inside, but something organic.

Something not so easily replaced.

This notion reminded her of Beckett and his finger that had been lopped off by the Church of Liberation.

She was recalling her last interaction with the enigmatic doctor when she nearly bumped into a man whose back was to her.

"Sorry," she grumbled.

The man turned.

"Chase? What are you doing here?"

Chase was as surprised to see Dunbar as he was to see her.

"Any update on our delivery man?" she asked, ignoring his question.

Dunbar shook his head and quickly led her to an unmarked room. Once the door was closed behind them, he turned on the lights and Chase found herself staring at the very man who had brought her Georgina's dress.

He looked much as he had earlier: disheveled, scared, and in need of a drink.

"No. I'm going to keep him a while longer, but he's sticking to his story about meeting a random guy at Barney's who handed him the box."

Chase grunted. She'd figured as much but had still held out a little hope that he might know more than he was letting on back at Oak Valley.

"Something tells me that that's not why you're here, though," Dunbar continued.

"Yeah—so we managed to get a positive ID on Glenn."

"Really? How?"

Again, she ignored the question for the sake of expediency.

"His name is Glenn Brick, and he used to be a patient at Oak Valley. Actually, he should *still* be a patient there… and would be, too, if Marcus Slasinsky hadn't broken him out."

Dunbar was incredulous.

"*What*? How the fuck did that happen?"

The security there is horseshit? The DA moved so many people around that nobody seemed to notice when one went missing?

"You recognize the name?"

Dunbar cocked his head to one side.

"Maybe. Gimme a sec."

The man plopped down in front of a computer and searched for Glenn's name.

"Shit," he said, pulling back from the monitor. "That's him alright. Arrested and charged when he was twenty-four for murdering two of his high school classmates. Was remanded to Oak Valley after an emergency psych eval."

Chase looked at the image of the man on-screen. There was something off about his appearance in the mug shot. All of his featured seemed… rounded, somehow.

"Anything else in the file?"

Dunbar clicked a button and then whistled.

"Forty-some pages."

Chase frowned. She didn't have time to go through that many pages.

"Who was the arresting officer? Can I speak to him?"

"Just a sec." Dunbar went back to the original file. "Damn."

"What?"

Dunbar tapped the screen and Chase read the name out loud.

"Detective Henry Yasiv… fuck. And he's AWOL, right?"

"Ever since the murder charges against him were dropped, no one has heard from or seen him since. His obstruction charges are still pending, but between you and I, I doubt he's gonna show up for the hearing. If you think people have strong feelings about Drake, double them and then you'll get an idea of Yasiv's reputation."

Chase was frustrated and annoyed now.

"Why is that all the fucking good cops get bad raps, huh?"

Dunbar shrugged.

"Let's see what I can do here."

The man started a deep dive into the paperwork before sighing again.

"I found another officer who helped then Detective Yasiv bring Glenn in."

"Good—let me talk to him."

"Yeah, that's going to be tricky, too."

"Why's that?"

"Because it's Officer Kramer."

Dunbar looked at Chase as if she should know the name.

"Dunbar, I don't have time for this. Who the hell is Officer Kramer? Is he dead?"

"Dead? No, he's not dead. It's worse than that: he's the one who wants Drake behind bars. He's the one who won't drop the goddamn charges."

Chapter 34

DRAKE SANK INTO HIS seat, wishing that Chase had parked anywhere but the 62nd precinct parking lot.

There had been a time when he would have walked through the front doors with his head held high. Even after he'd made numerous enemies by going after mayor Ken Smith and his minions, he'd remained unflappable. All that had changed, however, after his two stints behind bars. There was something about having your freedom revoked that was so inhumane that it bordered on torture. Drake's experiences had given him a new level of compassion for those behind bars… not all of the scumbags who had been locked up, of course, but those convicted of non-violent crimes, people who just got a shitty rap and didn't have the money for a proper lawyer, and the wrongfully convicted.

People like Marcus Slasinsky and Glenn Brick, though?

Torture maybe wasn't off the table.

Drake's thoughts eventually turned to the prison of guilt and self-immolation that Chase had built for herself over the years. Back when they'd worked together, it was clear that the woman had issues. At the time, Drake was also suffering from loss and had failed to notice the warning signs. While it was clear that they had both changed, when he'd seen the way Chase had been holding Georgina's dress in the trunk of her car, it was clear that she was still immured.

This, despite the fact that it was clear to both him and Dunbar—and Drake suspected Floyd and Hanna as well but had yet to ask them directly—that Georgina was *not* a victim here.

He knew full well that sometimes the only thing that held you back from doing what you needed to do to catch the bad guy was yourself.

And in this situation, with so much at stake, Drake knew that some difficult decisions had to be made.

He pulled his cell phone out and slowly scrolled through his contacts. It was a short list, one that was narrowed even further when the individuals who didn't wish him serious harm were excluded.

As much as Drake loathed the idea of going behind Chase's back, he knew how staunchly opposed the woman was to get the media involved. Although Chase claimed that her reasoning behind this decision was that Marcus might kill his captives if he found out they were on to him, this didn't make any sense.

On the contrary, everything that Marcus had done to this point was to let Chase know that he *was* involved.

Which meant that the real reason why Chase didn't want the press in the loop, whether she consciously knew it or not, was because she was still, after all these years, trying to protect her sister.

Loyal to a fault, was Chase Adams—something that Drake could relate to.

But that didn't change the fact that their most important job was to save Louisa and Stitts.

And bring Marcus Slasinsky and Glenn Brick to justice.

Georgina Adams, too, if it came to that.

Drake selected a specific contact and thumbed the call button. He was surprised that a male voice answered before the end of the first ring.

"I thought you were dead."

"I probably should be," Drake replied. "But I'm not."

"Then what do you want?"

"I think… I think I have a story that you might be interested in. I'm not ready to share the details just yet, but soon… very soon."

Chapter 35

"OFFICER KRAMER," CHASE SAID as she slid into the seat across from the young police officer. In front of her was a folder containing all of the information related to the Glenn Brick case. "My name is Chase Adams and I'm with the FBI."

The man leaned back in his chair, a smirk on his face.

"I know who you are. I also know that you used to work here."

Normally, Chase would've taken offense to the man's smug attitude and might even have put him in his place, but she decided to try a different approach for once.

"Yeah, well that's not what this is about. I'm here about one of your cases—one of your *big* cases."

Kramer was clearly suspicious of her quasi-compliment, but his ego soon took over.

"Which one? Because I've had—"

Chase removed Glenn Brick's photograph from the folder and spun it around for the man to see.

"Ah, that fuckin' piece of work. Yeah, I caught him. He would've gotten life if it hadn't been for his aunt."

Chase's eyes narrowed.

"Well, that's the thing. I'm trying to learn a little bit about this case, but I don't have much time. I would really, *really* appreciate it if you could give me the CliffsNotes on the case. If you can remember the details, of course."

Chase felt dirty tickling the man's ego like this, but it was a necessary evil. And she knew from her time as a Narc in Seattle just how to ply information from a man or to obtain a hit, depending on the circumstances.

"Oh, yeah, I remember. Shit, like I said, Glenn Brick ain't no Boy Scout, or Girl Guide, if you know what I mean. What do you want to know?"

Chase's eyes lifted to the clock on the wall above Kramer's head.

"Oh, as much as you can tell me in twenty minutes."

Kramer smiled, leaned forward, and interlaced his fingers.

"Twenty minutes? Oh, lady, I can do a lot in twenty minutes."

***

"Glenn Brick was born a twin—he had a sister named Glenda, but she died shortly after birth due to complications—don't really know the details there, couldn't find out much. Anyway, their mother, Callie Brick, also died during childbirth. But that was really just the start of Glenn's problems. He lived with his dad for a while, but it was clear that the man blamed his son for his wife and daughter's deaths—yeah, I know, hardly rational. But *Greg* Brick—yeah, fucking creative names this Brick clan—was more interested in the bottom of a bottle than fatherhood, let me tell you. Still, Glenn stayed with him and everything seemed all redneck hunky-dory until Greg lost his job when the boy was ten or eleven. That's when the beatings started—or, at least, that's when Glenn's teachers noticed the bruises. Cops quickly got involved and instead of owning up to what he'd done, Greg just took off. Nobody heard from him again—probably drank himself to death. Goddamn coward."

Chase soaked all this in, trying to ignore the man's ongoing commentary. She was interested in facts, not Kramer's opinions.

"What happened to Glenn next? Foster care?"

Kramer chuckled.

"Trust me, he would have been better off if that were the case—we all would have been. Instead, a nice aunt decided to look after poor Glenn out of the goodness of her heart. But, alas, as much as Daniela Shipley loved her nephew, she loved the checks that the state sent her as assistance every month a little bit more. During this transition, something fucked up happened. Believe it or not, even though Glenda Brick lived for less than a day more than a decade prior, some jerk-off in the records department decided that she *wasn't* dead and sent Daniela Shipley *two* checks a month, one for each Brick kid. Daniela didn't seem to mind—go figure. For more than two years this went on without anyone realizing that they were giving assistance for a dead kid. Eventually, somebody in the records department sobered up long enough to figure out that this was a mistake and sent a letter to Daniela saying that she would only be getting one check from here on out. That piece of work Daniela actually wrote back, if you can believe it. Claimed that Glenda *was* still alive and that she *deserved* the checks. So, what did they do? Well, some asshole from records went to check the situation out and, sure enough, he met Glenda. Well, not really. Glenn was on the slight side and a little effeminate, and Daniela decided to dress him up as a girl—to pretend to be Glenda. Classic move, never having the 'two' kids in the same room at the same time, I'll give Daniela that. And they bought it… for about a year. But, soon enough, a new records clerk noticed the discrepancy and went out to check again. Rinse and repeat, as they say. This worked fine until Glenn was about to turn thirteen… and I think we all know what happens then."

"Puberty," Chase said.

Kramer nodded.

"Yep. But Daniela Shipley, that kind-hearted woman, wasn't about to lose her social assistance checks just because of a simple technicality like puberty."

"What did she do?"

Kramer winced, the first genuine emotion that he'd shown the entire time he'd been telling his story, which was answer enough for Chase.

"You can't be serious."

"Yeah, dead serious. Daniela Shipley chopped the fucking kid's balls off just so that she could keep the ruse up. A real savage, that one."

Chase swallowed hard. Even though she didn't have the same equipment as Kramer, or Glenn Brick, just the idea of castrating a young boy was enough to curdle her stomach.

"After that, we don't really know what happened, but my guess? It was just easier for Daniela to start dressing Glenn up as Glenda pretty much all the time. And, let me tell you, from the images I've seen, Daniela was a little heavy-handed with the makeup. Really went all out in that regard."

Chase's heart started to beat a little faster as the pieces of the puzzle began to fall into place.

"Let me guess: white cheeks, red lips? That sort of thing?"

Kramer's brow furrowed.

"Yeah," he confirmed hesitantly. "Just like that. Anyway, Glenn or Glenda was also a little, ah, what's the PC term these days? Slow? I dunno—he had a little retard in him, let's just say. So, he was held back a few grades."

"Which is why he was twenty-three and still in high school."

Kramer nodded.

"Yep. To make a long story short, Glenn quickly found himself a target of some of the other kids and he dealt with it the way his daddy taught him: brute force. One day, Glenn snapped and killed two of his classmates. Then he painted their faces with that tranny-like makeup that his dear auntie used on him."

Chase had to consciously stop herself from shaking her head in disgust.

"Then what?" she looked down at the file, more for show than anything else. "You caught him, brought him in, and he failed his psych exam? Was deemed unfit to stand trial?"

Kramer chuckled again.

"Nope. He passed, if you can believe that—Glenn passed every fucking test he was given after being arrested. That's what I meant by saying he would've gotten life. But then, in the middle of the trial, his aunt decides to make an appearance. Just like that, out of the blue, she shows up, probably just got lost searching for her checks that stopped coming in the mail. Daniela Shipley wheeled her wheelchair right down the center aisle and plunked her fat ass there like she owned the place. Glenn saw her—everyone did—and something inside him broke. He immediately started talking in a high-pitched voice, claimed he wasn't Glenn, but Glenda. Judge called for a psych exam and he failed miserably. Personally, I think it was all a ruse, but the judge bought it—fuckin' bullshit. Still, it's not like he's free. Glenn Brick is gonna rot in that shithole Oak Valley for a *looong* time."

Chase just stared at Kramer for several moments after he finished speaking. Then, without saying a word, she packed up her things and started out of the room.

Before leaving, however, she turned back to face a confused-looking Officer Kramer.

"You sure about that?" she asked.

"What? About what? About Glenn? Lady, I was—"

"That he'll rot in Oak Valley? Because the last guy you sent there got out after just a few days."

With that, Chase left the office, offering Dunbar, who was waiting in the hallway, a curt nod to signify that she was done.

As predicted, Kramer rushed after her, only to be stopped by the Detective.

"Who? Who the hell are you talking about? Drake? You talking about *Drake?* Hey! *Hey!*"

Chase just smiled and kept on walking.

Chapter 36

CHASE GOT A MESSAGE just as she made it to her car. In the passenger seat, she saw Drake slip his phone into his pocket and silently urge her to get the hell out of here.

"Well?" he asked as she got inside. "You find out anything?"

Chase's eyes were locked on the message that she'd received from Floyd as she answered.

"Yeah, I found out that Officer Kramer is a piece of shit."

Drake chuckled.

"Could have saved you twenty minutes and just told you that myself."

Chase handed Drake the folder that Dunbar had given her about Glenn Brick and started the car.

"Check out the file and send a few snapshots of it to Floyd." Chase then tossed her phone at Drake. "And look at the picture he just sent me."

As she pulled out of the parking lot, Drake turned to her.

"This is the guy? Randy Kong? He's the guy who gave Georgina's dress to our delivery man?"

"Yep." Chase accelerated, pressing them both back against their seats.

"Where are we going?"

"To find this asshole, that's where."

***

"You sure you don't just want to go to this Randy Kong guy's house and wait there? He has to go home sometime," Drake asked.

Chase shook her head and continued to drive.

"According to Floyd, Randy is a regular at Barney's, which means that he's more than likely a drunk." She checked her watch. "Sun's going down… he'll be at a bar. Trust me. We just need to find the right one."

Drake fell silent, forcing Chase to look over at him.

"What? You want to just sit around and wait?" the words came out harsher than she'd intended.

"No, I don't. But this? Driving around and hitting up pretty much every skeezy bar in the neighborhood to try to find this guy? I can't help but think that we're once again back to following Marcus' breadcrumbs."

Chase's upper lip curled.

"Floyd is working on finding Glenn and I've got more than enough faith in the man. This is more… pressing."

Yet, despite her words, Chase felt more than a little uneasy about their approach. It wasn't just that Drake was probably right—that Marcus expected her to do just that—but they'd already visited half a dozen bars without anything to show for it. With the sun setting on New York City, the idea that they were wasting their time was creeping into Chase's mind.

What if Marcus already dealt with Randy Kong? What if he let Glenn loose on him and Randy was now just a corpse in an alley somewhere wearing that terrible makeup?

Chase was shaking her head to clear her thoughts when she noticed the characteristic flashing OPEN sign outside a squat, white building.

"One more," she whispered, more to herself than to Drake.

She pulled into the parking lot but was unable to find a spot on account of all the motorcycles that had parked sideways.

Frowning, she stopped her BMW right in front of the doors and hopped out.

"You can't park there, sweetheart," a biker with arms covered in tattoos informed her. He reached for her as she passed, but Chase slid by him.

"Hey, I'm talking to—"

Even though Chase hadn't turned to look at what had caused the man to stop mid-sentence, she knew that it must have been Drake.

There was something in Drake's eyes, something that hadn't been there before when he was still a detective, that would give anyone pause. It wasn't an old Western thing—it's not like Drake had a thousand-yard stare—but rather a blankness that was disturbing if nothing else.

Chase burst through the front doors, and then immediately wished that she'd been more subtle about entering.

The bar was full of bikers, every single one of whom was now staring at her.

There wasn't a single other woman in the place, so far as she could tell.

With the other bars, she and Drake had been more calculated in their approach. They'd flashed a picture to the bartender, a couple of servers, and asked if they'd seen Randy recently.

That wasn't going to work here.

Well, here goes nothing, Chase thought as she slipped her badge out of her pocket and held it high over her head.

"I'm with the FBI and—" several men started to rise while others crept toward the back door. She even saw one massive man start to reach around the back of his jeans as if grasping for a weapon. "—and I don't give a fuck about any of you. Seriously. I couldn't care less. All I care about is finding one man: Randy Kong. If you know him—"

Chase didn't need to wait for an answer, because she spotted him herself.

Randy Kong was near the back of the dive bar, half-seated on a pool table with badly stained felt. He first tried to shroud his face by pulling the hood he wore down, but Chase had already met his eyes.

"Randy!" she shouted, which was her second mistake since entering the bar.

Randy Kong got one look at her, turned, and started to run.

Chapter 37

"I THINK I'VE FOUND something," Hanna said.

Floyd, who had since returned to Oak Valley after retrieving security footage from Barney's, raised his eyes from his cell phone and blinked several times. He'd been reading the infinitesimal text that Chase had sent him on Glenn Brick for so long that his vision had started to blur.

"What is it?"

"Check this out." Hanna played a video that showed Marcus Slasinsky accidentally on purpose bump into one of the orderlies carrying a stack of files.

"I don't get it."

"Neither did I, until I slowed it down. Watch again."

Floyd leaned in close and spread his eyelids wide.

"He took a file. Marcus stole a file."

Hanna nodded and turned to face him. They were unexpectedly close, and a wry smirk appeared on her face.

"Sorry," he grumbled, pulling backward.

"No problem. But you're right—it looks like he stole a file. Can't tell which one, but…"

She held her hands up, indicating that she was going to keep looking.

Floyd needed a break from the atrocities performed on him by Glenn Brick, so as Hanna scanned more videos, he found himself unexpectedly chatty. He chalked this up to being exhausted, emotionally and physically, and also to the fact that Hanna was surprisingly easy to converse with.

"Is it true that you met Drake here, while you were working, and he was a patient?" he asked.

"Meh, I met him before that."

"Really? How long have you known him?"

"Long enough to know what a complete asshole he is," Hanna replied instantly.

Floyd was taken aback by the comment.

"Wh-what?"

Hanna looked at him, a smile on her face.

"I mean that in the best way possible. Drake is a colossal asshole, but only to bad people. To his friends, he's a lovable, loyal asshole."

It wasn't the answer that he'd been expecting, but it was answer enough.

"And when he and Chase were together were they, ah, *t-together?"*

Floyd cringed. He had meant to ask something else, but his fear of stuttering had changed the question from the time he'd formulated it in his brain to when it left his lips.

Hanna laughed, her bright eyes locked on his.

"I sense a little crush, Floyd."

Floyd felt his face grow hot and he averted his gaze like a kid who was just caught stealing.

"I'm just fucking with you—I have no idea. Probably not, though; I mean, he's resisted me for this long, so…"

Floyd looked up again, only to immediately return his eyes to his toes.

Hanna was attractive, there was no doubt of that, but she was also strange and complicated.

"You know that I fucked a serial killer once?"

"Wh-what?" Floyd's jaw went slack.

"Nothing—here check this out."

Thankful for the distraction, Floyd looked at the monitor.

Fucked a serial killer? Was she… serious?

In the video, a woman with dark hair that was shaved on one side walked down the hallway and then delivered a tray of food through one of the slots in a cell door.

And that was it.

"I-I-I'm sorry, I don't get it."

"That's me, Floyd," Hanna exclaimed with a hint of pride.

She looked different, younger, but it *could* have been her, Floyd concluded.

"Okay, but I still don't—"

"I just think I look good in scrubs, is all."

Hanna was staring at him again, and Floyd felt his face flush once more.

"You're cute when you're embarrassed, you know that?"

Floyd was so uncomfortable now that he nearly excused himself from the room, and probably would have, if it weren't for Hanna's next instruction.

"Keep watching."

"O-o-okay."

After the digital version of Hanna delivered the tray of food, she headed to another cell and looked around before opening it. The second the door was unlocked, a man stepped into the hallway.

A man who Floyd instantly recognized.

"That's Drake!"

"Yep—there's more."

Hanna led Drake to another room, a larger one with a single table inside, and then left him alone. When she returned, she brought another man with her.

"That's Marcus Slasinsky," Hanna informed him.

Floyd swallowed hard and tried to contain a new emotion that built up inside him: rage.

This was the man responsible for so much of Chase's pain.

Chase and Stitts'.

Hanna offered a running commentary as the video played.

"Long story, but I brought them together. Drake needed Marcus' help to bring down the mayor."

"Yeah, I-I know about that," Floyd said awkwardly. "But is there—"

"Easy, cowboy. There's more—just keep watching."

After a brief discussion, Hanna led Marcus to the common area and left him inside.

"Yeah, so shortly after this, Drake and I went for a little excursion outside the facility. But that's not what's important here. Watch Marcus closely."

In the video, Marcus entered the common area and went directly toward a man who was seated in a lounge chair, a book in hand.

They exchanged a brief hello and then Marcus said something that made the man's face and posture suddenly change. The man in the chair pursed his lips, and he crossed his legs, knee over thigh. He even seemed to sit up a little straighter.

"I guess now we know what file Marcus stole," Floyd said softly.

Hanna made a face.

"What? How? That there is Glenn Brick."

Floyd shook his head.

"No, it's not, it—"

"Naw, I'm pretty sure. Look at the features. That's Glenn Brick in the chair."

Floyd started to smile, realizing that the tables had turned; it was Hanna's turn to be embarrassed. Or confused.

"No, it *was* Glen Brick. But now? After Marcus said whatever he said? Now, it's *Glenda* Brick."

Chapter 38

RANDY KONG WAS DRUNK, and Chase was determined. She reached the man right before he slammed into the emergency exit. Instead of trying to grab him, though, she reached out with her foot and clipped the back of his right heel. Randy's legs pretzeled and he spilled into the alley.

Chase followed, ignoring the shouts from bar patrons behind her.

"Who gave you the package?" she demanded.

Randy's face was a bloody mess from striking either the door or the asphalt and the only answer he could manage was a moan.

Chase pulled out her gun and rolled Randy onto his back with her foot. The man's eyes were bulging, and blood trickled from both nostrils and ran into his mouth.

"Who da fuck are you?" he mumbled.

"The box with the dress in it. Where did you get it from?"

Randy turned his head to one side and spat blood.

"It was—"

"What the fuck's goin' on over there?" a gruff voice demanded.

Chase swung around to see a burly man approaching in a sweatshirt and smoking a cigarette. Two other bearded men flanked him.

"FBI," she said, holding up her badge with her free hand. "Back the fuck up."

This did not have the desired effect; either they couldn't read her badge, or they simply didn't care.

"You can't hit him like that. Let the man up."

They continued to approach, and Chase had to fight the urge to raise her gun. Experience taught that aiming her pistol at civilians never ended well. Especially when said civilians were more than likely armed, themselves.

"Back up," she ordered.

"The FBI can't be—"

A fist came out of nowhere and connected with the leader's jaw. A shower of sparks from the cigarette between his lips accentuated the blow and there was an audible crack as his teeth mashed together.

The man's eyes rolled back, and he collapsed into a puddle.

"What the fuck?"

The other two men's surprise lasted only a moment before they started to back away.

"She may be FBI," Drake said as he stepped from the shadows, "but I'm not."

Chase gawked.

She hadn't even seen him step out of the bar, let alone slide down the alley before cold-cocking the biker with the beard.

Chase shook her head and turned back to Randy who had since managed to pull himself into a seated position.

"Where did you get the dress from?" she asked again.

"Some hooker."

Chase moved closer, raising her gun to hip level—not quite aimed at Randy, but not exactly aimed away from him, either.

"You're going to have to do better than that."

Randy spat blood again.

"I don't know her fucking name, all right. Never even seen her before. Some goddamn ugly ass hooker just came up to me in the street and said she would pay me a thousand bucks if I took it to some fuckin' address in the boonies. That's it. Shit, I didn't even do it—I gave someone five-hundred to take it out there."

Chase grimaced. The story sounded made up, which, knowing Marcus Slasinsky, probably meant that it was one hundred percent genuine.

"Why did you even bother? Why not throw the box in the trash and keep all the money for yourself?"

"I don't fuckin' know."

Chase raised the gun a couple of inches.

"Fuck, okay, the goddamn hooker creeped me out, all right? Said she'd find me or some shit if I didn't make sure it was delivered."

Even though Randy's story seemed to match up with the man from Oak Valley's recounting, Chase still held out hope that he was holding back.

He *had* to know more, for Georgina's sake.

"What was her name?" Chase asked. "The hooker?"

"You fuckin' deaf? I just said—I don't know." Randy probed his nose and whined. "Shit, I think it's broken."

Chase had had enough. She raised the gun and pointed it at Randy's chest.

"If you don't tell me her name, it's going to be more than your nose that's broken. Who gave—"

A hand came down on the barrel of her gun and gently lowered it.

"We should get out of here," Drake said. When Chase hesitated, he hooked his chin over his shoulder. "The biker's waking up."

Chase turned back to Randy and clenched her jaw.

"If you think that a hooker was going to hurt you, if I find out you're lying—"

"I'm not fucking lying!"

"Come on, let's go," Drake said.

"I'll come back for you, if you're lying, I'll come back," Chase finished.

The back door to the bar opened and three large men tried to squeeze out at the same time.

"Who the fuck—"

Chase didn't even hear the end of the sentence; Drake grabbed her arm and together they ran.

Chapter 39

"ANSWER THE PHONE, CHASE," Floyd mumbled. After what he'd seen in the video, and explaining Glenn Brick's history to Hanna, he'd tried desperately to reach Chase and tell her what he'd found.

But she'd gone AWOL.

He just hoped that she was with Drake and didn't have another breakdown, another relapse.

"Not pickin' up, huh?"

"No."

Hanna punched the gas. She drove like an absolute maniac. In fact, Floyd, who was familiar with the inner workings of most mechanical objects, was unsure how her VW, aged as it was, could actually move the way she made it go.

Twice, he had to put down the cell phone and grip the handle on the ceiling to ensure that he didn't fly either into the center console or out the window.

The other issue was, Floyd didn't actually know where they were going.

When Hanna pulled out her own cell, which made Floyd grip the handle even harder and squeeze his ass cheeks even tighter, he finally found out.

"Dunbar, it's Hanna—yeah, I'm with Floyd. We're coming to you."

Floyd gave her a look to which Hanna responded with a shrug.

"No, no way—I'm not going inside. You have to meet us in the parking lot."

Hanna took a hard left, nearly forcing Floyd up against the window.

"Two minutes. Yeah."

Hanna hung up then lowered her cell phone.

"You ready for this?" she asked with a grin.

"No."

"Good. Hold on tight."

True to her word, Hanna pulled into the 62nd precinct parking lot two minutes later. Floyd's stomach caught up with them thirty seconds after that.

It was dark now, which made a random car pulling into a police lot and nobody getting out even more suspicious. Thankfully, Dunbar noticed their vehicle and hurried over.

Hanna rolled down the window.

"Dunbar, Marcus planned all this shit when he was back in Oak Valley," she said without preamble. "We have him on video speaking to Glenn Brick and we're pretty sure that he was recruiting him as far back as six months ago. Maybe longer.

Dunbar, who was clearly overwhelmed by Hanna's excitement, leaned down and looked at Floyd.

"Yeah, she's right," he confirmed. "We think that he learned about Glenn's whole... *situation*... and used that to manipulate him."

"Shit."

"Hey, Chase wouldn't happen to be here, would she?" Hanna asked.

Dunbar shook his head.

"No, she was here a few hours ago, but haven't heard from her since."

"Probably out looking for Randy," Hanna mumbled.

"Who?"

"We managed to find out who gave the box with Georgina's dress to the guy you have in custody and sent that information on to Chase," Floyd explained.

Dunbar's face changed; although he wasn't technically in charge, it was clear that he was annoyed that he hadn't been kept in the loop.

"Has he said anything, by the way? The guy who delivered the package."

"Nothing—one of my guys will continue to sweat him for a bit, but then I'm cutting him loose. He doesn't know anything."

"Shit," Hanna said. "Well, that fucking sucks... dead end there, Chase and Drake are nowhere to be found... what the hell do we do now?"

It took Floyd several seconds to realize that both Dunbar and Hanna were looking to him for a suggestion.

"Well, I-I-I mean, we can always look for R-Randy...?"

Hanna's expression soured.

"I don't know Chase, but I know Drake. He probably already has the guy in a headlock." Dunbar made a noise and Hanna quickly backpedaled. "Figuratively, of course."

"I guess we can expand the search for Glenn, get a few more uniforms out there, comb the streets," Dunbar suggested. "Floyd, any update from the FBI on where the photo of Stitts and Louisa was sent from?"

Floyd didn't reply—he was lost in thought.

Searching for Randy was the wrong move. As was doing what Dunbar had just suggested: a random grid search for Glenn and Marcus.

Marcus was simply too smart to be picked up that way.

He had to remind himself that he was no longer just a driver for Chase or the FBI. And yet, he wanted to be *the* driver—as in the driving force behind this operation.

You're a bona fide FBI Agent, Floyd. Act like it.

"I'm not sure, but..."

Hanna stared at him, her face blank and Floyd just let his sentence trail off.

For some reason, he didn't want to let the woman down. Maybe it was because she was attractive and had flirted with him back at Oak Valley, or maybe it was the fact that Floyd saw a parallel between Hanna and Chase.

Whatever the reason, he didn't want to be the old Floyd anymore. The old Floyd would have succumbed to the pressure on him now, broken down into a stuttering mess, and deferred to a signpost.

But that was before saving both Stitts and Chase's lives on a rooftop in Washington.

That was before he'd brought the drone to Chase in Albuquerque.

Dunbar opened his mouth to offer another option, but Floyd held up a finger.

Think... neither Chase nor Stitts are here, which means that you're the one in charge.

Floyd closed his eyes.

Stitts...

Stitts was the profiler, the one who came up with the plan of attack, which Chase acted out.

What would he do? Floyd wondered.

He tried to conjure up an image of the man's face to help inspire him, but every time, Stitts had white makeup on his cheeks and red lipstick smeared across his mouth.

And then there were the butterflies...

"The scene of the crime," Floyd suddenly blurted.

Hanna looked at him as if he'd just thrown up on himself.

"What?" she and Dunbar asked in unison.

Floyd was about to second guess himself but took a page out of Chase's book and allowed his subconscious to fill in the blanks… and prevent him from stuttering.

"These killers, these murderers? They almost always return to the scene of their crimes, to the places that mean the most to them."

"You mean that after years in Oak Valley, Glenn gets out and now feels… what? Remorse? Guilt? Wants to pay homage to his victims?" Dunbar asked, not even bothering to hide his obvious skepticism.

"No," Floyd said flatly. "Not because of anything like that. It's because they want to relive the murders, they want to try to recreate the feelings that they experienced."

Dunbar blinked.

"You sure?"

"I'm sure. These killers can't resist going back to the scene of their crimes."

Hanna surprised Floyd by clapping him on the back.

"Thatta boy, Floyd."

Dunbar still looked skeptical but eventually nodded along with the PI.

"Well, you're the one in charge…" he looked at Hanna. "But there's no way I'm getting in a car with Hanna. Just wait a minute while I grab my own vehicle. Then, Floyd, you lead the way."

Chapter 40

"SO, WE'RE JUST GONNA keep cruising the streets, looking for a tall, ugly hooker?" Drake asked.

"Yep, that's exactly what we're going to do," Chase replied, her eyes scanning the sidewalk. She would stay all night if she had to. All week or as long as it took to find the woman who'd given Georgina's dress to Randy Kong.

"What about talking to some of the beat cops? They usually know all the regular working girls. If we had them helping us out, we could cut out—"

"No. No more people, Drake."

Chase pulled over the side of the road and rolled down the window. A woman in fishnet stockings with brown hair that fell to her shoulders emerged from the shadows. Her leather crop top was so tight, and her breasts forced so high, that she was in real danger of suffocation.

"You lookin' for something?" Her voice was huskier than Chase suspected, which took her by surprise.

"Yeah, I'm looking for a box."

The woman smiled.

"Oh, yeah?"

Drake leaned out the passenger window.

"Not that kind of a box."

The woman, noticing Drake for the first time, immediately stopped smiling and took a cautious step backward.

"I don't do couples."

"It's not like that," Chase said, shooting Drake a glance. She dangled her hand out the window, a folded hundred-dollar bill pinched between her first two fingers. "I'm looking for information about a box."

The woman looked at the money, then Drake, then Chase.

With a shrug, she stepped forward and snatched the bill from Chase's grasp.

"You're going to need to be more specific."

Chase was relieved and disturbed at the same time.

This is how easy it is to lure women into your car, even if you have a suspicious-looking man seated beside you. This is how Lance O'Neill managed to do it, with Tessa Greenfield's help.

Chase was transported back into the Devil's Den and she shuddered as if Lance had shocked her with the cattle prod again. The prostitute must've misinterpreted this gesture, because she crossed her arms over her chest, a not-so-easy task given her immense bust.

"You change your mind? I don't do refunds."

"No, no refunds. I'm looking for a street worker who handed a box off to a friend of mine." Chase called up the photo of Randy Kong on her phone and showed it to the woman. As she did, she saw that she had more than a dozen unread messages and numerous missed calls but dismissed the notifications.

The woman, still hesitant, pushed her chin toward the phone but remained at a comfortable distance.

"Never seen him. And I don't know about no box, neither."

Chase cursed and the woman got defensive.

"No refunds," she said quickly.

"No, I know, I know," Chase rubbed her brow.

The prostitute sighed.

"What kind of box? Like cardboard one? It'll probably help if you tell me what was *in* the box." Her tone was softer now.

"Yeah, a cardboard box. The thing is," she cast a quick look at Drake, "my wedding dress was inside. It's a long story, but, shit, I guess I owed somebody some money and they used it as collateral. I know, I know—it's not really worth anything, but as you can see, I can pay for it now. I—*we*—really want it back."

There were more holes in her story than Swiss cheese, but it was the best Chase could come up with on the spot.

The prostitute leaned down to get a better look at Drake, then made a face.

"You two are married?"

"N—" Drake began but stopped when Chase elbowed him in the ribs.

"Yeah, going on three years. Anyway, this guy here? On the cell phone? I gave it to him, and he said he gave it to one of you girls."

The prostitute was incredulous.

"A wedding dress? Listen, lady, a lot of Johns try to pawn off some shit when they can't afford to pay, but a *wedding dress?* You sure that this guy gave it to a street worker?"

"Honestly? I don't know. That's what he said. I mean, he turned down all the cash I owed him and more."

"Well, I'll tell you what: you have a picture of that guy? If you do, I can pass it around, see if any of the girls recognize him. That's the best I can do."

Chase frowned and mulled over their options. She didn't have a printout, all she had was the photo that Floyd had taken from the security footage at Barney's.

"You really think that someone might remember him?"

The prostitute grinned.

"Someone who paid for services with a wedding dress? Lady, if it happened, I'll find out about it. We talk to each other, you know. It's the best way to stay safe in this business."

Chase was taken aback by the comment. She'd heard something similar in Albuquerque. The problem wasn't that they didn't talk, it was that some girls chose not to listen.

And it cost them dearly.

"Take it, then."

"Take what?"

"My cell phone. Take it and show the picture to some of your friends."

"Chase," Drake said.

Chase nudged him again.

"You sure? That's—"

"How about, instead, you give her your cell phone number and she'll send you the pic," Drake offered, ignoring Chase's protest this time.

The prostitute nodded.

"Yeah, okay, sounds good. Just because it's sentimental."

She rattled off her number and Chase quickly sent the prostitute the picture. Then she produced another hundred-dollar bill and handed it over.

"If you hear anything, please, just give me a call."

"Sure thing." With that, the woman backed into the shadows once more.

Satisfied that they could accomplish nothing more here, Chase pulled away from the curb and started to drive.

She'd told Drake that she didn't want any more people involved in the search for her partner and sister, but the prostitute clearly belonged to a different world.

They'd made it about half a block before Drake spoke up.

"You're welcome."

"For what?"

"For letting you keep your cell phone."

Chase scoffed.

"How the hell was I supposed to know that the prostitute had a cell phone? Hell, how did *you* know?"

Drake looked at her.

"I know this prostitute named Veronica, and you wouldn't believe the stuff she's told me…"

Chapter 41

FLOYD HELD ON FOR dear life as Hanna raced out to Leeside High School. Of course, they beat Dunbar there—even in his unmarked police car, he had no chance keeping up with her.

As they sat in the dark with their lights off awaiting the detective's arrival, Floyd's eyes kept drifting from the two-story building to Hanna.

Imbued with newfound confidence, Floyd started to wonder if her flirting was specific to him, or just something she did with everybody.

"See something you like?"

And just like that, the fickle nature of confidence was revealed.

"S-s-sorry," Floyd grumbled, quickly looking back at the high school.

Even though his rationale was solid, something wasn't sitting quite right with him. The school was dark, apparently locked, and there were no signs of movement from within. Part of him wanted to call up Dunbar and say, forget it, this was a mistake. That they should wait for the real pros like Chase or...

Stitts.

In his mind, Floyd saw his friend bound to a chair, his mouth covered in grimy duct tape.

"There's a janitor waiting for us."

Dunbar's voice made Floyd jump. He hadn't even seen the man approach in his car, let alone on foot.

"Let's go."

Hanna got out of the car and Floyd followed.

When Floyd spotted a man in a dark tracksuit standing by the front gates—a man whom Floyd hadn't seen even though he'd been staring at the building for a considerable amount of time—his hand slowly started to move toward the butt of his gun.

"Detective Dunbar?" a voice with the thickest New York accent that Floyd had ever heard asked as they approached.

"You must be Colin Saldano," Dunbar replied, holding out his hand.

"That's me, since the day I was born." Instead of shaking Dunbar's hand, he held out a keyring that looked straight out of the 1800s.

"Yeah, I know. We tried those fancy electronic door keys, but the damn things kept messing up." Colin sorted through the keys and separated two from the rest. "This one here's for the front, while this one, the one with the big black *D* on it, is for the back door."

The man chuckled, as did Hanna, but Dunbar remained stoic. He reached for the keys, but at the last second, the janitor pulled his hand back.

"I need to see some ID first."

With a sigh, Dunbar produced his badge. It was almost impossible to read the damn thing in the poor lighting, but the man nodded and then turned to Hanna next.

"Seriously?"

With a head shake, Hanna showed her PI badge.

"Now you."

Floyd was so flustered by this whole charade that it took several tries for him to get his badge out. And when he eventually succeeded, it was upside-down.

"Sorry," he said, turning it right-side up.

"All right, now I don't like to go to bed much later than midnight, so do your best to be done by then. Give me a call, and I'll come get the keys. But like I told you on the phone, detective, nobody's been here since I left at eight."

"Sure, I understand. I also appreciate you keeping this to yourself," Dunbar said.

"Alrighty then, knock yourselves out."

With that, Colin left, and the three of them headed through the open gate and made their way to the front door. Dunbar got there first and peered through the glass.

"Floyd, why don't you go around back."

Floyd swallowed hard and looked at Hanna.

"I'm not waiting out here. Fuck that."

"She stays with me," Dunbar said in a tone that suggested that this was non-negotiable.

"Well, I could go by myself if you jackasses had let me go back to SLH Investigations and get my gun."

Floyd was secretly happy that Dunbar had kyboshed that idea. Hanna was reactionary and unpredictable, and the idea of her with a gun was a little alarming, to say the least.

"Brought you a flashlight," Dunbar said. "Both of you."

Floyd took his and checked to see that it was working.

"Jesus," Dunbar said, immediately shielding his eyes.

"Sorry," Floyd said, immediately flicking it off.

Dunbar pulled out his phone.

"All right, it's eleven-oh-four now, let's meet back here, at these doors, no later than eleven-thirty. Floyd, you start from the back and work your way forward. Hanna and I will clear the second floor. If you see anything, just shout out or flash your light three times. That cool?"

"Yeah," he lied. "Cool."

One final nod and a wink from Hanna, and Dunbar unlocked the front door.

"What if—" Floyd began, but the two of them were already inside the building.

—*We find him?* He meant to ask. *What the hell do we do then?*

Chapter 42

"EVEN YOU ARE GOING to run out of money if you keep handing it out like that," Drake remarked.

It was a cool night, but he enjoyed having the window down and the fresh air in his face. Even though the smell of New York City left something to be desired, he missed these odors a little. If nothing else, it just felt familiar whereas the Virgin Gorda was forever foreign.

And he missed *this*, too; for so long he'd been working alone. He missed working with Chase, someone who had nearly as much experience as he had.

Someone he didn't need to protect.

Someone equally as damaged as him, if not more.

"Good thing I've got a rich benefactor backing me," Chase said.

It was the closest thing to a joke that had come out of her mouth since she'd gotten him out of prison.

"Yeah? And how'd you manage that?" Drake asked playfully.

"I needed a backer for a poker tournament where someone was murdering the players and stealing their money."

Right, not the joking type.

"I see."

They fell into silence again, which made Drake uncomfortable. His thoughts tended to turn to either his deceased brother or Jasmine and his child, the latter of whom he'd seen for less than an hour since being born.

Chase slowed and pulled over to the side of the road after spotting a female silhouette near the mouth of an alleyway.

Without hesitating, she pulled another hundred out of her bottomless wallet and held it out the window.

Drake wondered now, sincerely, where all this money was coming from.

Is the FBI just giving her cash?

He shook his head.

Stop being an idiot—it's her poker winnings that are funding this.

"Hey," Chase said softly. "I just have a quick question for you."

The woman stepped forward and Chase's posture became more rigid. There was a red welt encircling the woman's right eye.

"You okay?" Chase asked, her tone hardening.

The woman sniffed and wiped her nose with the back of her arm. As she lowered her arm, Drake noticed a series of swollen red dots in the crook of her elbow.

"Please," the woman sobbed. "You need to help me. My pimp… he beat me up and I'm scared."

From his vantage point, Drake had a clear view of the woman's face and, despite the fact that her tears were real, the woman's eyes were cold and flat.

Chase reached for the door handle.

"Where is he? Where's your pimp?"

As Chase started to open the door, Drake reached out and grabbed her arm.

Something didn't feel right about this.

She turned to look at him.

"What are you—"

"Bitch, give me that hundred and everything else you got," a male voice demanded.

Drake let go of Chase and sank deeper into his seat. Beside the woman now stood a man in an oversized New York Mets jacket.

"You hit her?" Chase asked.

The man spread his legs and reached for the butt end of a pistol that jutted out from his low-hanging jeans.

"Bitch, you hear me? Gimme that fuckin' money."

The man was so focused on Chase that he didn't even see Drake slowly worm his way out his window all the while drawing his gun.

As Chase continued to argue with the thug, who was becoming increasingly agitated, Drake sat on the window frame with his legs inside and his elbows on the roof of the car. He aimed his gun at the center of the man's forehead.

"Keep your hundred, Chase."

The man's eyes shot up and he noticed Drake for the first time. He tried to play it cool, but when he saw the gun, he swallowed visibly.

"You even know how to use that thing, old man?"

Drake said nothing; he just stared.

"I bet you ain't never shot nobody before. Why don't you just—" the man tried to pull his gun, but it got stuck.

"I'll shoot you dead before you get that thing out of your fucking pants," Drake informed the thug in the deadpan voice.

The man's eyes darted from Drake to the girl who had started this whole setup. She was no longer crying and instead focused her efforts on trying to pull the thug away from the car.

It was all a ruse.

"Come on, let's get the fuck out here. It's late and I'm hungry."

The man sneered.

"You're one lucky motherfucker, you know that?"

Drake watched the couple leave, tracking them with his gun. It wasn't until Chase nudged his leg and told him to get back into the car that he animated.

"Should have shot him," Drake muttered.

"Okay, Wyatt Earp," Chase said, rolling her eyes.

Drake looked over at her and was surprised to see that she had drawn her gun, as well. It was resting on her lap, aimed through the door at what would have been crotch level for anyone standing on the sidewalk.

"Was that a joke?"

Chase shook her head.

"Maybe. Maybe it—"

Her phone buzzed and Chase immediately jammed her gun down the side of her seat and picked it up.

"Well, I'll be damned."

"Who is it?"

"It's that hooker—she said she wants to meet up."

"What did she—"

Before Drake could even finish his sentence, Chase put the car into drive and he nearly fell out the window.

Chapter 43

You wanted this, Floyd. *You wanted to be in the FBI, now deal with it.*

His thoughts were meant to soothe him, but they did the opposite: they made him even more nervous.

The interior of the school was dark, much darker than Floyd would've imagined. He'd expected some sort of emergency lights to at least lead the way, but there was nothing. Thankfully, the tactical flashlight that Dunbar had given him acted like a floodlight, but now, with his pupils dilated, everything outside the beam was pitch black.

He crept slowly down the hallway, listening to the sound of his own breathing, trying to pick up any other noises in the otherwise silent building. Rows of lockers reflected his light, as did the classroom windows, which had a disorienting effect.

If a student had returned to collect a forgotten textbook, he had no doubt that the kid would have been in serious jeopardy of being shot.

Thankfully, Floyd didn't see another soul.

With every empty classroom he passed, he expected his anxiety to wane.

It didn't.

Instead, it was like playing a game of Russian roulette: the more times the gun didn't fire, the greater the chances that the next trigger pull would be deadly.

Sweat broke out on Floyd's forehead and he wiped it away with the back of his hand. Just as he was lowering his hand, he heard a banging from what seemed like directly above him. Floyd idiotically aimed his flashlight at the ceiling and held his breath until he heard faint footsteps.

It was just Hanna knocking something off the table; that was it. It wasn't Glenn Brick cutting them with a knife or anything like that.

Floyd allowed himself a deep breath and then picked up the pace as he continued down the hallway. Eventually, he found himself at the front doors, having seen no sign of Glenn Brick.

He was relieved but also disappointed.

Laying the flashlight on the barrel of his gun, he pulled out his phone and checked the time.

Eleven-oh-eight? How the hell—

"Fl—"

The sound came out of nowhere and Floyd swiveled, raising the gun and flashlight combo to eye level.

He was just taking aim at an approaching figure when the flashlight slipped in his sweaty hand and fell to the ground.

"—oyd! Jesus Christ, Floyd! Put the gun down!"

His heart was pounding so hard in his chest, that Floyd thought it might burst through his rib cage and land on the floor, destined to become a specimen in anatomy class.

"You almost shot me!" Hanna exclaimed as she bent down to pick up his flashlight. She attempted to hand it to him, but Floyd was trembling too much to take it.

"I'm-m-m-m-m-m-m-m—" *sorry*, Floyd meant to say, but he couldn't formulate the words.

Hanna giggled and gently guided his still raised gun out of the way by pushing his forearm.

Her skin was cool, much cooler than his own, which was boiling hot, and her touch seemed to snap him out of his stupor.

"Shit, I'm sorry. You just, uh, well, I'm just a little freaked out."

Hanna moved closer and wiped the sweat off his brow.

"You're a bit of a spaz, aren't you?"

Floyd was about to defend himself when he saw that she was smiling.

Then Hanna did something completely unexpected. As she pulled her hand away from his forehead, she pressed onto her toes and kissed him on the lips.

Floyd recoiled as if he had been struck.

"Wh-wh-wh-what are you doing?" he stammered.

Hanna laughed again.

"Relax—you need to calm down, Floyd. You need to—"

"Hanna! You were supposed to stick with me," Dunbar reminded them as he hurried down the hallway toward them.

Hanna handed the flashlight back to Floyd.

His mind was racing, trying to figure out what the hell had just happened. One minute he'd nearly killed Hanna, the next she was kissing him.

"Yeah, got bored. Look, he's not up there—c'mon, we all know that."

Dunbar stepped into the beam from Floyd's flashlight.

He didn't look pleased.

"Nothing upstairs. You find anything down here, Floyd?"

"No. Nothing."

"What about down there?" Hanna asked, pointing at a set of large red doors tucked into an alcove to their left. Floyd aimed his flashlight in that direction and read the words beside the door out loud.

"Boiler room."

Oh, shit.

Only bad things happened in a boiler room.

Hanna bounded ahead and reached for the thick chain looped between the metal door handles.

"The lock's off," she said.

Floyd stiffened again.

Please, we're not going down there…

But it appeared that that that was precisely what they were going to do.

Dunbar nodded at Floyd.

"I'll go first, Hanna, you stay in the middle, while Floyd, you take the rear. Got it?"

***

The boiler room was a thing of nightmares, complete with spiderwebs as thick as rope. But it was the sounds that were the worst: random clicks and clacks and hissing like the noises of a prehistoric beast.

Or perhaps of a demented eunuch.

Thankfully, the boiler room wasn't very large, and many of the areas were simply too small and cramped for a man of Glenn Brick's size to hide out in.

"No sign of him," Floyd said, trying to sound brave, trying to keep the fear from his voice.

He failed miserably.

"Yeah, it doesn't look like even our janitor friend has been down here in some time," Dunbar said in a matter-of-fact tone.

"What a fucking bust," Hanna piped up.

"Alright, let's get the fuck out of here. We can—"

"There's something there behind the boiler," Floyd interrupted, his eyes focusing on a large shard of glass that lay on the ground. Unlike the rest of the random items in the room—a piece of wood, an old classroom clock, the boiler itself—the shard of glass was curiously devoid of dust or grime.

Floyd leaned around the back of the boiler and spotted where the glass had come from: there was a broken carrying case with a plastic handle on top nestled just out of sight.

He reached down and picked it up. Several other shards of glass fell, but he ignored them.

"What is it?" Hanna asked, moving closer.

"Looks like some sort of carrying case," Dunbar offered.

"Yeah, but a glass one?"

Floyd wasn't positive, but he thought he'd seen something like this before.

It looked to him as a sort of mobile habitat that one might carry butterflies in.

Or maybe he was just biased by their search for the Butterfly Killer.

"Could be to transport butterflies."

Hanna and Dunbar exchanged looks and shrugs.

"You sure?" Dunbar asked.

Floyd shook his head.

He wasn't sure. The only thing he was sure of was that it was an empty, broken case of some sort.

"Maybe." He looked at it for a moment longer before lowering back to the ground. "Can't be sure."

"It doesn't matter," Dunbar, the voice of reason, stated. "Even if Glenn Brick or Marcus Slasinsky were here, they're not here now. Let's go back up."

Floyd didn't need to be asked twice.

Once outside, all three of them breathed in the cool, fresh air.

"So much for your theory," Hanna said. Floyd couldn't tell if she was truly disappointed, or if she was just teasing him again.

"I thought… I thought that Glenn would come back here, to the scene of his crimes. You sure this is the right place?"

"Positive," Dunbar replied immediately. "Two bodies—one upstairs, one on the main floor."

Their throats slit, their faces painted with makeup, Floyd thought with a shudder.

"What about the field?" Hanna asked.

"What field?"

"The field that Mike Brian or whatever his name was found in. Maybe we should check there?"

Floyd thought about this for a moment.

While violent serial offenders, such as Glenn Brick, liked to return to the scenes of *all* their crimes, the location that had the largest impact on them held the greatest importance.

And the Mike Brian kill seemed more of a Marcus Slasinsky-inspired murder than Glenn Brick's idea.

"Worth a shot out, I guess," Dunbar conceded. "It's not far from here."

Hanna and Dunbar started toward their respective vehicles, but Floyd remained rooted in place.

An idea had entered his brain and had taken hold.

The place that holds the greatest importance...

"Floyd? You coming?"

Floyd didn't respond, didn't move.

For most murderers, the location of their first kill inspired the greatest emotion.

But Glenn Brick wasn't like most killers.

A knot began to form in Floyd's gut.

"Earth to Floyd... you want us to leave you here?"

"No, it's not right," he whispered.

"You second-guessing yourself?" Hanna asked. "You think our boy Glenn Brick just hiked up his skirt and hightailed it out of New York?"

"No, no, I don't think so."

"Then what, Floyd? Where the hell do you want us to go?" Dunbar exclaimed. For the first time, the man allowed emotion to creep into his voice. "We can't just stand out here waiting for something to happen. We need to—"

"No, not the place Glenn first killed. The place where he was *castrated*."

The words came out without a hint of a stutter.

"What?" Dunbar gawked.

Floyd suddenly became emboldened.

"He's not coming back here to the school, and he's not going to the field. He wouldn't even consider returning to Oak Valley."

"He's going to his aunt's house," Hanna said excitedly. "That's the place that means the most to him, that's the place where his life got royally fucked up."

Floyd nodded and he allowed himself a small smile.

"Yeah, that's exactly where he's going."

Chapter 44

CHASE TRIED TO TEMPER her excitement as she returned to the site where she'd initially met the prostitute with the huge breasts and fishnet stockings.

Even though the woman's message had been cryptic, she had high hopes that she had figured out which street worker had seen the dress.

From there, she would grease the wheels once more, which would hopefully lead her to Marcus and her sister.

It was a slog, it was slow going, but at least it was *moving*.

"Slow down, Chase," Drake said.

"I am going slow," Chase replied. She took a sharp right so hard that the wheels of her BMW squealed on the pavement. "All right, all right, I'll slow down."

But Chase didn't press the brake; she simply let her foot off the accelerator a little.

Nearly two days had passed since she'd first received the photograph of Louisa and Stitts and the only thing that had happened since was that three people had died.

Chase recognized the spot from earlier in the night and pulled over so hard that her front wheel bumped the curb.

Drake grunted but held his tongue.

Instead of waiting for someone to emerge from the shadows, she opened the door and got out of the car.

Behind her, she heard Drake follow.

"Hey, have you seen—" Chase began, addressing the first prostitute that she saw. She paused when she realized that she never actually got the woman's name who was on the lookout for Randy Kong.

And yet, the prostitute whom Chase was addressing seemed to know who she was talking about and stepped into the light.

"Heather," she said while looking over her shoulder. "Heather, the short lady who was looking for the dress is here."

The dress... my wedding dress...

Chase reminded herself of the story that she'd invented and handed this new street worker a hundred-dollar bill. The woman inspected it for a moment but took it and then disappeared. As if they were the same person, only in different costumes, as soon as the first hooker vanished, Heather appeared, a cigarette dangling from between cherry red lips.

"What have you found out?" Chase asked as she hurried toward the woman. "Do you know where the dress came from?"

As she neared, however, Heather's expression changed. She took a drag from her cigarette, flicked the ash the ground, and said, "Nothing."

Chase's heart sunk.

"What? Nothing? What do you mean, *nothing*?"

Heather crossed her arms over her breasts.

"I'm sorry, but I asked everyone I know. Nobody traded a wedding dress for services—nobody even has a clue as to what I was talking about. Nobody has seen your guy, either."

Chase ground her teeth.

"You asked everybody? Bullshit," she looked down at her cell phone. "It's barely eleven-thirty. How could you have asked everyone already?"

The woman stared blankly at Chase.

"As I said before, we talk to each other out here. No dress. I warned you that I probably would have heard about something like that. This one time, the man tried to give me a Mont Blanc pen for a hand job. Like what the hell would I do with—"

"I don't care about your fucking pen," Chase snapped. "I want the dress that one of you hookers gave to Randy Kong!"

Heather took a step backward and pursed her lips around her cigarette.

"I thought you said it was the other way around; I thought your man gave it to one of us." As she spoke, the cigarette moved up and down almost hypnotically.

"Chase," Drake said from behind her.

"He gave her the dress, she gave him the dress, what the fuck does it matter? I need to know where it came from."

"I don't know what to say, lady," Heather said, emphasizing the final word. "Must've been a new chick, because none of the regulars know anything about a dress."

Chase threw her arms up.

"Fuck," she exclaimed. "Fuck!"

Drake wrapped an arm over her shoulder. Normally, Chase would have shrugged off the help of any man, but Drake wasn't just *any* man.

Besides, she'd reached her breaking point and simply collapsed into him.

"Here, take this," she heard Drake say, and somewhere in the back of her mind, she realized that he'd removed the hundred-dollar bill from her hand and was offering it to Heather. "And thank you for your help."

"Yeah, thanks, and I hope you find your wedding dress."

With that, Drake gently guided her back toward her BMW. By the time she got there, she was practically nestled into his chest. Somehow, he got her into the car and then sat beside her in the passenger seat.

They sat in the dark with the vehicle off for several minutes.

And then, Chase started to sob. It didn't take over her whole body, didn't send her into seizure-like tremors, but it was all-encompassing nonetheless.

Instead of saying something placating, clichéd, or trite like "It'll be okay, everything will be okay," Drake simply held her.

After the sobs passed, Chase wiped her nose and then looked up at him.

"They're going to die, Drake; Stitts and Louisa and Georgina are going to die, and it's all my fault."

PART III – Makeup and Butterflies

Chapter 45

"For fuck's sake," Dunbar grumbled, his eyes locked on his phone.

"What's wrong?" Hanna asked, pausing half in and half out of her car.

"The fucking delivery guy is asking for a lawyer. Looks like we're going to have to cut him loose."

"So what? Let him go—he doesn't know anything."

Dunbar frowned.

Floyd found this interaction interesting: a PI giving an NYPD Detective advice on his own prisoner. But that was the thing about Hanna; her unwavering confidence demanded respect.

"Yeah, I know—I know. But I gotta get back, sign some papers."

"Why? Get one of your minions to do it."

Dunbar shook his head.

"I checked him in, I have to check him out. You guys…"

Dunbar let his sentence trail off and Floyd quickly chimed in.

"We'll head to Glenn Brick's aunt's house. Catch up with us there."

From the expression on Dunbar's face, it was obvious that this wasn't the answer he'd wanted, but Floyd was technically in charge. And yet, deep down, Floyd *wanted* Dunbar to protest—he was still reeling from nearly shooting Hanna in the high school—but he also knew that Stitts was out there somewhere.

And his friend needed him.

In the end, the detective nodded.

"Alright—please, let me know if you find anything."

It took Floyd close to thirty seconds to gather the courage to get into Hanna's car. It wasn't just the idea of encountering Glenn Brick again that frightened him, but the woman's driving, as well.

The latter fear was borne out in mere minutes.

"You really think he's gonna be there?" Hanna asked as she sped away from the high school. "I mean, this Daniela Shipley broad, she messed him up good."

Floyd briefly tried to get a read on her, to figure out if she was poking fun at him after wasting their time at the school or if she was genuinely looking for more information.

It was impossible to tell.

"I-I think."

"Just brimming with confidence, huh," Hanna shot back, her eyes not leaving the road.

Floyd blushed. He was about to say something that, provided he could manage words that weren't completely mangled by his stutter, would have undoubtedly embarrassed him further when Hanna took a sharp left. Floyd braced himself to avoid being slammed against the window.

"Sorry, sorry," Hanna whispered. "Didn't see the pothole—it's dark out."

"Ye-yeah, it tends to do that at night."

Hanna chuckled.

"All right, funny guy, hold onto your hat."

***

"You sure this is the place?" Hanna asked as she turned off the lights and peered through the windshield.

Floyd had to wipe the perspiration from his brow and eyes before getting a good look at the building. After riding with Hanna, the possibility of running into Glenn Brick here was something of a relief.

The address that he'd pulled from Glenn Brick's file as his last known residence panned out, but he was skeptical, none-the-less. The building, which was set back from the road, might have once been painted green. Now, it was a dull gray, and what paint remained after what had to be years of neglect was peeling off in monochrome strips. The roof was only half-covered with shingles, and based on the way it sagged in spots, the interior likely had its fair share of leaks.

The single window on the second floor was cracked, but there was a light on inside, confirmation that the house still had power, at least.

Floyd squinted, trying to make out a shape or form in that window, but the spiderweb shatter made it impossible to identify anything concrete.

"This is the place… I guess after Daniela stopped receiving the welfare checks for Glenn and Glenda, she didn't have money for repairs. Anyway, Glenn could be here."

"*Could*," Hanna repeated. "Yeah, maybe. Just in case, you got that gun with you?"

Floyd checked his hip out of habit, even though he'd felt the butt dig into his side with every bump Hanna drove over.

"Yep."

Hanna stepped out of the car and then closed the door quietly. Floyd did the same and went to her side.

"You wanna give it to me?"

Floyd pulled back and looked at the woman.

"Wh-what? What do you mean?"

Hanna giggled and slapped him in the belly.

"I'm just fucking with you. You're cute when you're scared, you know that?"

Once again, Floyd blushed.

They stood there in silence for several moments before Floyd realized that Hanna was waiting for him to make the first move. He got the impression that it wasn't because she was scared—he didn't think Hanna was frightened by anything—but because she respected him.

Floyd took a deep breath, unclipped his holster but kept the gun inside, and then started forward.

"All right, I guess we… just knock on the door?"

He immediately cursed himself for making the sentence sound like a question.

You're the one in charge here, he reminded himself. *Act like it. And no more blushing.*

"Sounds good."

Floyd did his best to step over the rotted boards that made up an anemic front porch and then pulled out his badge.

"Stay behind me," he instructed.

"Sure thing, boss."

Floyd found a section of the wooden door that wasn't soft to the touch and knocked three times.

"Someone's moving upstairs," Hanna said after the echo from Floyd's knock died down. "In the room with the light."

Straining, Floyd thought he could hear someone coming down the stairs. They waited and eventually the door opened just enough for an eye to peer out.

"Sorry to bother you at this late hour, ma'am. My name is Floyd Montgomery and I'm with the FBI." He flashed his badge, hoping that the woman sporting the blue eyeshadow could read it in the dim light. "And this here is my... colleague. I was hoping that you could answer a few questions for me."

The woman pulled back far enough that Floyd had a hard time making out her eyes. He was reaching for the flashlight that Dunbar had loaned him when she finally spoke.

"What do you want?" Her voice was hoarse and scratchy.

"You wouldn't happen to be Daniela Shipley, would you?"

"What do you want?"

I'm guessing that's a yes.

"We're here inquiring about your son, about Gl—"

"I don't got no son."

"Your nephew, Glenn," Hanna corrected as she slid in front of Floyd.

Son? You idiot.

"Yeah, Glenn—we're wondering if you could tell us the last time you saw him."

"That little pussy is behind bars. I ain't seen him in a long time." With that, the woman started to close the door, but Hanna blocked it with her foot.

Daniela Shipley scowled and stared down at her running shoe.

"What about your niece?"

"My niece?"

Floyd was annoyed by the way the woman repeated every question they asked. It was a classic stall tactic if he'd ever seen one.

"Yeah, Glenda. When's the last time you saw her?"

The woman suddenly straightened, and Floyd had to look up to maintain eye contact.

"What do you want?"

Floyd opened his mouth to say something, but Hanna had taken the reins and wasn't about to let go anytime soon.

"Tell me where Glenn is, you sick fuck. How could you—"

Floyd instinctively reached for Hanna, but she'd anticipated this and dodged his grasp.

"Get off my property."

Hanna didn't listen.

"You castrated a young boy, and now he's out there killing people. I bet you feel as guilty as—"

Floyd finally managed to grab a hold of Hanna. He pulled her away from the door and they both stumbled on the warped deck. The second her foot moved from the threshold, the door slammed closed.

Hanna turned to him and made a face.

"Well, that went well," she remarked.

Floyd shook his head and led the way off the weather-beaten porch.

"Should we call Dunbar? Get him to come here and bust down the door? Or can you just do that? Being the FBI, and all?"

"I don't think—" Floyd paused, his eyes drifting back to the door that was still quivering in its hinges. "I don't think he's here."

Hanna stared at him, incredulous.

"Really? A half-hour ago you were certain of it."

Floyd sighed.

"I-I-I don't know. I thought… maybe? But that was before I saw Daniela Shipley. I doubt that they would be living in harmony given what she did to him."

Hanna's mouth moved to one side of her face as she thought about this.

"Well, can't we just kick down the door, anyway? She is a sick fuck, after all."

There was no doubt about that, but they still had rules and a protocol to follow.

"No, we can't—we have no PC or warrant. Imagine the press if she decides to call the media."

Hanna stared up at the house.

"I doubt she even has a fucking phone." After a short pause she added, "Fine—what do we do now, then?"

The high school idea had been a bust, as had been visiting Glenn's aunt. As much as Floyd wanted to be in charge, to prove his worth, it was about time that he deferred to someone with more experience.

"I have no idea. But I think I know who does… if only she'd answer her damn phone."

Chapter 46

"**I THINK... I THINK** your phone is ringing. *Again.*"

Chase took a deep breath and wiped the tears from her eyes. She tried to center herself by thinking about Dr. Matteo and the techniques that he'd spent hours upon hours teaching her.

In the moment... Stay in the moment, Chase. Be present.

She shook out her arms and then grabbed her cell phone.

It was Floyd and this time she answered it.

"Floyd? What's going on? Tell me you've got some good news because we've reached a dead end here. The trail of breadcrumbs ended at Rodney." She paused to give Floyd a chance to answer, but when he didn't say anything, Chase looked at the phone to make sure she hadn't accidentally hung up. "Floyd? You still there?"

"Yeah, I'm still here. B-but, unfortunately, I-I-I don't have good news, either. We went to Glenn Brick's original crime scene—the high school where he killed those two boys."

"And you didn't find anything."

"N-n-nothing."

With a heavy sigh, she pulled the phone away from her ear and set it on speaker so that Drake could listen as well.

"That's it? Floyd, I'm—"

"And then I thought Glenn would go back to his aunt's house, given what she did to him. She was here, but—"

"—the dumb cunt doesn't know anything."

Chase looked at Drake.

"Who's that?"

"Hanna. As I was saying, we went to Daniela Shipley's house thinking that Glenn might have returned here, given that this was the place he was castrated. The house is such a disaster that we didn't think that anyone lived here, at first, but there was a light on upstairs. Anyways, we knocked, and she came to the door."

"And? Did she seem surprised to see you? Like she was hiding something?"

"Not... not really. She just kept repeating our questions back to us. I don't... I don't think he's here. I can't imagine the two of them living together after what she did to him."

Chase's mind went back to the scene that Officer Kramer had described to her. About how when good ol' Aunt Shipley had rolled herself into the courtroom and once Glenn saw her, he immediately became Glenda. Sure, he'd undergone therapy for years after this incident back at Oak Valley, but Chase knew firsthand that some habits were hard to break.

Impossible, even.

"You didn't see anyone else inside?" she asked, grasping for straws now.

"No—the woman barely opened the door before slamming it in our faces."

Chase looked to Drake for something to add, but the man appeared as lost as she was. So much for their old-fashioned detective work. So far, all trails leading to Marcus ended at a brick wall.

"You want me to go back and... talk to her again?" Floyd asked hesitantly.

"Hey, the light just shut off." Chase heard Hanna say. "If we want to talk to her, we better do it before she chases her Valium with some prune juice."

"No, I think—" Chase's brow knitted. "Wait, did you say that the light in the house was on *upstairs*?"

"Yeah—second-level."

"And it's an old place?"

"Old? More like ancient."

Chase's mind was whirring now as she replayed Officer Kramer's story over and over again.

"Floyd, when Daniela Shipley answered the door, did it look like she was sitting down?"

"Wh-what? Sitting down? Why would—"

"Yeah, Officer Kramer said—"

"Fu-fu-fu—"

Chapter 47

"—**FUCK,**" **FLOYD FINALLY MANAGED** to spit out.

"What? What is it?" Hanna asked.

Floyd ignored her and looked at the second-floor window, the light of which was off, as Hanna had just said.

"Chase, y-you should get here as soon as you can."

He hung up and swapped his phone for his gun. The whole time, Hanna was staring at him as if he'd lost his mind.

"What the hell is going on, Floyd?"

"Wheelchair," he said, starting back toward the house. "Stick behind me."

When he realized that Hanna wasn't following him, he turned back.

"Glenn's aunt is wheelchair-bound. The woman who answered the door moments ago? She was taller than me."

Hanna's brow lifted, then quickly fell.

"Shit," she whispered. "Shit!"

"Yeah, let's go."

This time, Floyd didn't knock on the door. This time, he raised his boot and delivered a hard kick just beside the handle. The door was so rotten that the frame itself split and it fell inward. He flicked on the flashlight and stepped inside.

"Glenn! Glenn, I know you're in here!"

The interior of the home was silent.

"FBI! Glenn, get down here!"

Floyd swept the room on their right first, or at least he tried to; it was so completely full of magazines and stacks of paper and trash that it was nearly impossible to determine if somebody was buried beneath the refuse.

He moved toward the kitchen next, the counters of which were piled high with filthy dishes but stopped when he reached a carpeted stairway.

Pushed to a decision, Floyd elected to head upstairs based on the light they'd seen flick on and off earlier. He took the stairs two at a time, wincing with every creak, half-expecting to fall through and into the basement.

"Glenn!"

The first bedroom was empty, as was the bathroom. Moving with his gun and flashlight trained in front of him, Floyd approached the room with the broken window.

"Glenn, come out with your hands up."

His breathing quickened as he neared the partly closed door.

"Last chance, I'm going to—" he pushed the door open with his free hand midsentence, hoping to take Glenn by surprise. "—hands up! *Hands up!*"

There, in front of a vanity with a mirror so dirty that it was rendered opaque, was a woman in a wheelchair, her back to Floyd.

"Glenn, put your hands up. It's over."

As he cautiously moved forward, Floyd observed the man's hands that dangled down the side of the wheelchair. The fingernails were manicured and the fingers themselves were shorter than he would have expected considering how tall Glenn was.

"Glenn?"

Floyd reached out and grabbed the woman by the shoulder and spun her around. The chair moved fluidly enough, but he wasn't prepared for what he saw.

Floyd stumbled backward, nearly falling right out of the room.

It wasn't Glenn seated in the wheelchair, but Daniela Shipley and her throat had been slit from ear to ear. The woman's wrinkled face was covered in thick white makeup and her lips were redder than the blood that soaked the front of her nightgown.

"Fuck," he moaned as he scrambled to his feet. It was only then, as he swung the flashlight around frantically that Floyd realized Hanna hadn't stayed behind him as he'd instructed.

"Hanna!" he yelled. "Hanna!"

Driven by fear, Floyd hurried back down the stairs. He'd made it halfway before the door at the back of the kitchen swung open and a figure rushed out.

"Hanna! He's getting away!"

Floyd leaped over what looked like the corpse of a dead cat and sprinted toward the door. His shoulder struck it before it fully closed, and he was launched into the night.

In his mind, he imagined hitting the ground running, barely breaking stride, as he pursued the demented murderer.

But that plan was foiled immediately. There was no back step, and it was a good three-foot drop from the kitchen to the muddy ground below. Somehow, Floyd managed to roll with the fall, thus preventing any serious injury, but in order to do so, he had to let go of both the flashlight and his gun.

Hanna! He's getting away! You have to stop him! Floyd meant to shout, but he was still struggling to catch his breath. To his right, he spotted his gun and scrambled toward it only to stop when a foot came down beside it, followed by a knee.

Floyd was about to roll away when a face lowered to his level.

It wasn't Glenn or Glenda Brick.

It was Hanna, and she was smiling.

"Drop something?"

Floyd grabbed her outstretched hand and allowed the woman to help him to his feet.

"He got away!" he nearly moaned. "Glenn got—"

"No, he didn't."

Hanna sprayed his flashlight on a body slumped in the mud; the man's legs spread, his hands lying limply at his sides. Floyd looked at Hanna, who was flipping what appeared to be the handle of broom in her hand like some sort of experienced busker.

"Glenn didn't get away, Floyd. He's just taking a little nap."

Chapter 48

"WUH-WUH-WE SHOULD CALL DUNBAR," Floyd suggested.

"No, we should wait for your partner," Hanna countered. "But first, give me a hand here, would you?"

Together they managed to drag Glenn's tall but waif-like body back into the house. Then they sat him on a chair and tied his arms and legs with some twine they'd rustled up from one of the overflowing kitchen drawers.

Their handiwork was a notch above shoddy, but Floyd figured with the two of them there, and the gun back in his possession, the man wasn't going anywhere.

Only once they were satisfied, did the two of them step back and observe the man more closely.

"You know, his makeup isn't that bad," Hanna remarked. Floyd, while by no means an expert in the field, had to agree. Unlike his victims, Glenn wore immaculate blue eyeshadow and his cheeks were lightly blushed. His pale pink lips matched the shade of nail polish on his fingernails.

The man was also wearing a nightgown that looked very similar to the one that Daniela Shipley sported upstairs.

"He probably made her do it before he killed her," Floyd said absently.

Hanna recoiled.

"What?"

"Oh, shit, I found his aunt in the bedroom." He didn't need to say more. At first, Hanna expressed shock, then she sneered.

"Bitch got what she deserved."

Floyd bit his tongue.

Did she?

He wasn't about to argue that the woman hadn't done horrible, unthinkable things, but clearly, she suffered from severe mental illness.

Nothing else could explain her actions.

Except, perhaps, greed.

"We should call Dunbar," Floyd repeated.

"No, we should wait for your partner. Especially now that you told me about the dead psycho upstairs. If Dunbar comes, he's gonna have to call it in. That means that weird ME, uniforms, all that jazz. The place will be crawling with cops. Then what are the chances that we can get Glenn or Glenda to talk?"

Floyd raised an eyebrow. What Hanna was suggesting went against all SOPs, but she did have a point.

"I wonder how—"

Hanna hushed him.

"Quiet, he's waking."

As if responding to her voice, Glenn's head rolled to one side and his eyes started to open. With blue eyeshadow flickering, his face suddenly hardened.

"What do you want?" Glenn said in the same voice that he'd used when Floyd and Hanna had first knocked on the door.

"What we want, is for you to tell us where Marcus Slasinsky is." Hanna stepped in front of Glenn and squatted. Glenn responded by trying to raise his arms and Floyd was relieved to see that the rope, which had been looped through the back of the chair, held.

"I don't know who that is."

"Come on, Glenn, the act's up. I mean, that's some good makeup you got going on, but we know it's you."

"I'm not Glenn," he said, his lips twisting into a sneer. "Glenn's a pussy, a faggot. That boy… he ain't good for nothing."

Glenn tilted his head to one side, revealing a bloody dent just above his ear.

Jesus, how hard did she hit him?

"Glenn, Glenn, Glenn. Maybe I need to give you a whack up the other side of your head to clear your thoughts a little bit." As she spoke, Hanna picked up the broomstick and twirled it in her hand.

Floyd knew that he should take it away from her, but he was mesmerized by the way it spun in her palm.

"I'm not Gl—"

Hanna stopped spinning the stick and grabbed it with both hands. When she started to swing it like Barry Bonds in his prime, Floyd had no choice but to intervene.

"Hanna—"

But Hanna stopped just short of making contact without Floyd having to do anything. Glenn, however, convinced that he was going to be struck again, whipped his head to one side. When he realized that there was no blow forthcoming, he turned back to face Hanna.

Only now his face had changed. It was softer, younger, somehow.

"Please, don't hurt me again," Glenn whimpered. His voice was no longer that of a crotchety old woman but high-pitched, young and naive.

Hanna cast a confused look over her shoulder at Floyd, who shrugged.

So far as he knew, there was no FBI handbook on how to deal with someone like Glenn Brick.

"Please."

"Glenn, stop this—" Hanna began, but was interrupted.

"My name's Glenda—Glenn's my brother."

"Sure, you are. You need to tell us—"

Glenn pouted.

"It's true, it's true I swear it. My name's Glenda."

Hanna changed tactics and used the end of the broom not to strike or prod the man, but to slowly lift the hem of his nightgown.

"You sure about that, Glenn? You want me to check under the hood? Because even though you talked a big game back at Oak Valley, I guarantee that I have bigger balls than you do."

The man's face changed a third time. His eyes became wide and his grin grew to almost comical proportions.

When he started to laugh, a horrible titter, Floyd shuddered.

"Ah, Jesus, stop that," Floyd said. But his words only seemed to encourage Glenn. His laugh got louder, and he turned his chin to the ceiling. "Jesus, make him stop."

"Glenn, shut the fuck up," Hanna implored.

The laughing increased in both pitch and cadence.

"Shut up!"

When he still wouldn't stop, Hanna took the stick in both hands.

"You want me to hit him?" she asked with a shrug. "You want—"

Floyd was about to answer when a figure strode into the house and ripped the stick from Hanna's hand before she could react.

"No, that's alright—I'll do that. I'll hit him."

Chapter 49

AND THAT'S EXACTLY WHAT Chase did.

She swung the broomstick in a sharp downward trajectory and made contact exactly where Glenn's collarbone met his shoulder.

The laughing immediately stopped. After Glenn stopped grunting in pain, he focused his eyes directly on hers.

"Who the—ah, it's you. The one he's always going on about."

Chase glowered at the sick bastard strapped to the chair in front of her.

"Yeah, it's me. I'm guessing you didn't get me mixed up with Hanna this time, did you?"

Glenn looked at Hanna before coming back to Chase.

"Not this time," he replied with a small grin. The man's voice—his *real* voice—was slightly high-pitched, but it had a masculine quality to it, nevertheless.

"No more games. Where is he?"

Glenn didn't answer right away. Instead, his eyes drifted over Chase's shoulder.

"And you? Well, what do you know, it looks like the whole gang is here."

Chase knew that Glenn was referring to Drake, but Hanna and Floyd seemed surprised by his presence. The former even went as far as to walk over to him and give him a hug.

"Glenn, I'm going to give you one chance to answer the goddamn question. I want you to tell me where he's keeping Stitts and Louisa. If you don't tell me, I will hit you with this fucking stick again."

"You mean where *she's* keeping them."

Chase gripped the broomstick so tightly that her palms started to ache.

"*Him*: Marcus Slasinsky or Dr. Mark Kruk or whatever alias he's going by now. I want to know where he's keeping them."

Glenn chuckled.

"You mean where *she's* keeping them. The girl with the orange hair."

The simple mention of her sister was enough to set her off. Chase brought the stick down even harder this time in the same spot as before.

Glenn howled and threw his head back and then immediately struggled against his bindings.

They held.

"I want to know where Marcus is keeping them," Chase said again, her voice flat and even.

"You mean—"

Chase swung the broomstick again, not once this time, but three times in rapid succession, the third time so hard that it cracked somewhere deep inside.

Glenn screamed, and when Chase pulled the stick away his left shoulder now hung much lower than the right.

"Tell me where he is."

"Chase, maybe—"

Chase didn't even know which one of her colleagues had spoken, but she didn't really care.

"One chance. Tell me."

"I don't know," Glenn said from between clenched teeth. "I don't know where he is."

Chase hit him again and this time Glenn just moaned.

"Bullshit. Where are they?"

"I don't know! I don't—"

Glenn fell silent when Chase raised the stick in both hands. Before she could let loose another blow, someone grabbed the end and yanked it. Her hands were so slick with sweat that it slipped from her palms.

She turned, expecting to see Drake holding the bloodied broomstick, but was surprised when she saw it in Hanna's grasp.

"His shoulder's numb. I think we should work on the knees next."

Without waiting for confirmation, she reared back and delivered a blow so hard across Glenn's kneecaps that his chair almost toppled.

The man let loose a piercing howl.

Chase watched this display in awe; she knew the moment she'd met Hanna that the woman was tough, but this was next-level shit.

It was good to know that she had someone like Hanna on her side. And it was reassuring that Drake had Hanna to look out for him for when Chase wasn't around.

"He comes to me, I swear. He just... *shit*... Marcus just messages me when he wants something done."

Chase raised an eyebrow.

"Messages you? On what? A cell phone? You have a cell phone?"

Glenn nodded.

"Where is it?"

"It's... it's..."

Hanna pointed the stick at his chest and the man swore.

"It's there—I put it in the top drawer in the kitchen. Was trying to get it when you guys busted down my door."

Chase looked at Floyd and cocked her head toward the kitchen. The man hurried across the room and tore open several drawers. He returned less than a minute later with an archaic-looking flip phone in hand.

"Go through it," Chase instructed. "See what's on there."

Floyd did as he was instructed.

"We've got texts from just one number—all just a bunch of times and dates."

Chase nodded and turned her attention back to Glenn.

"Yeah, that's him. That's Marcus; they just told me where to be and when. That's it. Everything else he—"

"—told you back at the psychiatric facility," Hanna finished for the man.

Glenn swallowed hard.

"Floyd, reply to one of the most recent texts. Pretend you're Glenn and tell Marcus to come here, that he needs to meet up."

When Floyd didn't raise his eyes from the cell phone, Chase started to get worried, thinking that perhaps it wasn't just times and dates.

That maybe there was a picture on the phone, one that included Stitts, Louisa, and, of course, Georgina.

"Floyd?"

Floyd looked up.

"What's wrong?"

"M-m-m-maybe we should talk about this for a moment," Floyd replied, looking over at Drake. Drake appeared to understand what the man meant and together they stepped forward.

"Talk about what?"

Floyd's eyes darted from Drake to Chase and then to Glenn.

"I-i-in the other room, before we send a text."

Chase felt her frustration mount. They had no way of knowing if Marcus' captives were still alive, and yet Drake and Floyd wanted to waste time talking about the wording of a damn text?

But she knew, based on their mirrored expressions, that this was non-negotiable.

"Fuck," she swore. She glanced over at Hanna. "Keep an eye on him... if he moves, hit him again. This time, aim for his head."

Hanna smiled.

"Shit, it would be my pleasure, FBI lady."

Chapter 50

"I DON'T KNOW IF sending a text message is the smartest thing we can do right now," Floyd said, his eyes locked on the cell phone in his hand.

"What are you talking about? We don't have time to waste… if we send Marcus a message, he won't be able to resist; he'll come running if he thinks that I'm here, that I've been captured," Chase said quickly.

Floyd looked up.

"Yeah, maybe… but he didn't show up at Oak Valley when he thought you were there," Floyd reminded her.

"That's because I *wasn't* there. Or maybe Glenn tipped him off."

"Not with this phone," Floyd said, holding up the cell he'd taken from the kitchen drawer. "No outgoing texts. Not one. All incoming, all just times and dates."

"What's your point?"

"My point is, Marcus has been leading us along this whole time… he probably knew that we'd come here, that we'd eventually find Glenn. I mean, it's not like he was hiding out in another state."

Chase sneered.

"Or maybe he's not as smart as we think he is. Maybe we're finally out ahead of Marcus and every minute we stand here talking is just—"

"Chase, I think Floyd's right," Drake offered. "Glenn didn't send a text when he thought he grabbed you and me back at Oak Valley, so why would he text him now?"

Chase threw her hands up.

"Well, what the fuck then, Drake? Floyd? I'm not going to just sit around in this shithole waiting for Marcus to send another goddamn message."

"I can get the FBI to run a trace on the number used to send Glenn the texts," Floyd said. "Maybe—"

"Like they traced the picture that Marcus sent me of Stitts and Louisa? Huh?" Chase clenched her jaw. "This is bullshit."

Floyd looked down at the phone hoping for a suggestion of what to do next to materialize.

"We need to make Marcus want to come to see Glenn," Drake said, taking Floyd off the hook. "That's the only way."

"Gee, thanks, Columbo. How the fuck are we going to do that?" Chase snapped. When Drake scowled, she averted her eyes. "What's the next step in Marcus' master plan? Does Glenn even know it? Or is his part done?"

Both Drake and Floyd fell silent. So far, Glenn had led them to the cell phone that Marcus used to contact him with, but that was it.

Floyd let his eyes drift back to the man in the kitchen whom Hanna was guarding. The side of his head was bleeding, and his shoulder was drooping, but his makeup was strangely perfect. Even if they could beat more answers out of him—of which Floyd wasn't positive—did he even know anything of value? Marcus had been so careful with the rest of his plan, what with having a series of random people pass Georgina's dress on before it got to them, it would be awfully careless to share incriminating information with someone as unstable as Glenn.

"Nothing? That's just—"

A thought suddenly occurred to Floyd.

"I think we all agree that M-Marcus has been running the show up until now, that he's been pulling the st-string. There's only one thing that the man wants, the rest—Louisa and Stitts? Glenn? Georgina's dress?—they're all just a means to an end."

"Chase," Drake said immediately. "That's what he wants; he wants you, Chase."

"Yeah, I know. Sick fuck is obsessed, no thanks to you. I'd gladly give myself up in return for Stitts, Louisa, and Georgina. Shit, I'd do it in a heartbeat if I thought he'd let the others go. But even if—"

Floyd shook his head.

"N-no, see that's the thing: that's what he expects you to say, to do. That's what he's u-u-using against us, to st-stay one step ahead. We need to do the opposite."

"What the hell is the opposite of giving myself up?" Chase asked, her face awash with confusion.

"Take you away," Drake stated.

"What? Take me away?"

Floyd was nodding and a small smile crept onto his face.

"What would piss Marcus off the most? If he *couldn't* have you."

"Really? This is your plan? Put me into hiding? WitPro? He'll just keep coming for me, we *know* this. He's obsessed. Drake, can you talk some sense into Floyd here?"

"No, I think he's right."

Chase grunted.

"Of course, you do. You guys—"

"But you're right, too. Marcus *would* keep coming. Unless you're somewhere he can never get to," Floyd continued.

"What?" Chase's voice rose an octave, and, in his periphery, Floyd saw both Hanna and Glenn turn in their direction. "I doubt there's a place on planet Earth that he wouldn't look, eventually."

"Exactly."

Chase rolled her eyes.

"Oh, I see, you're talking the *moon*? Like a—"

Drake looked to Floyd and nodded.

"We're not talking about a place, Chase. We're talking about killing you," Drake said flatly. "You want Marcus to come to Glenn? Then we take away the thing he wants most in this world: we let the man kill you."

Chapter 51

DESPITE THE FACT THAT it had been Floyd's plan, and even though Drake was fully on board, he was still uneasy.

But it made sense. To take control away from Marcus, they had to make sure that he could never have Chase.

And there was only one way to do that, permanently.

"Looks fucking horrible," Hanna remarked. "But I guess that's the point."

Floyd concurred.

Chase's face was covered in white makeup, sloppily applied like all Glenn's other victims. Her lips were bright red.

"Yeah, that's pretty close," Drake said. He'd been the one to go take a look at what Glenn had done to Daniela Shipley to make sure that the makeup was a match. And yet, he didn't seem happy about the results. Everyone in the room, it seemed, was on edge, Chase included.

She was seated in a chair across from Glenn, whose mouth was taped shut so that they didn't have to listen to either his psychotic cackle or him switching seamlessly from Glenn to Glenda. Hanna, who had applied the makeup, was tilting her head to one side as she inspected her work. Drake's arms were crossed over his chest, while Floyd held Glenn's cell phone in one hand.

"No, something's wrong here," Floyd said unexpectedly.

Chase looked at him.

"What? What is it? What are we missing?"

Floyd felt his ears get warm.

"All the other victims…" he let his sentence trail off, opting instead to draw a circle over his chest with a finger.

"The butterfly," Drake said. "You're missing the butterfly."

Chase appeared to be contemplating her options but eventually nodded.

"Hanna, ask Glenn where he keeps the blood."

Hanna tore the tape off Glenn's mouth, and he cried out.

"Where's—"

She didn't even need to finish the question; after all, the man's mouth had been covered, not his ears.

"Upstairs, in the vanity drawer."

Hanna patted him patronizingly on the head and then reapplied the tape.

"I'll get it," Drake offered, already making his way toward the stairs.

During the interim, Floyd walked up to Chase and looked at her intently.

"You sure you want to do this, Chase?"

"It's your plan—shit, I'm not really dead, Floyd. If this means finding Stitts and Louisa? Georgina? You're damn right I'm sure."

Floyd was about to add something else when the phone in his hand buzzed.

"What the hell?"

Chase sat bolt straight.

"Is that his phone? Glenn's phone?"

Floyd stared at it for a moment, but when the buzz returned, he realized it wasn't Glenn's phone, but his own in his pocket that was making the noise.

"No, it's mine and it's Dunbar calling. For the... shit, the fourth time."

"Don't answer it," Drake said from behind him. Floyd turned to see a small vial with a purple cap in his hand. In the bottom were maybe a few drops of blood.

Blood that Stitts had given to Drake.

Floyd kept this little tidbit of information to himself.

"Yeah, but he's not an idiot," Hanna said. "He knows we're here, and he's going to come looking for us."

"Eventually," Drake concurred, holding the blood out to Hanna. "You know what the butterfly looked like?"

Hanna took the vial.

"Yeah."

"You do it then." To Floyd, Drake said, "Give her the cell phone."

After Floyd handed it over, Drake picked up Glenn's chair with the man in it and turned him around to face the wall.

"All right, Hanna, draw it here." He pointed at his sternum. "When you're done, send the picture. We'll be right outside the room."

Drake grabbed Floyd by the arm and together they stepped into the hallway.

As they continued toward the front room that was full of musty magazines, Floyd overheard Hanna in the kitchen.

"All right, you ready for this, Chase?"

Chapter 52

"IS SHE… IS SHE gonna be okay?" Drake asked.

The question surprised Floyd so much so that he struggled to answer. After all, Drake would know if Chase was going to be okay, wouldn't he?

He swallowed hard.

"I've seen her come through worse," Floyd replied honestly. And he had seen Chase come through worse. He had seen her near-death at the bottom of a quarry, wearing nothing but a pair of soiled underwear. And yet, what he didn't add, is that his reply depended on whether or not her friend, her partner, and her sister came out of this unharmed.

"You need to look out for her, Floyd," Drake said. "This thing with her sister…"

Floyd nodded, stemming his sentence midway through—the man didn't need to say the rest.

Floyd knew it, Drake knew it, and Hanna knew it as well. Dunbar, too.

Her sister wasn't a victim here, she was Marcus' partner. And when Chase finally came to this realization, there was no way of telling how she would react.

"I'll do what I can, Drake."

It was a weak answer, but it was better than nothing. And Drake seemed to accept it. They both knew Chase, knew how much of a loner she was, how all of the problems of the world were on her shoulders. Her work with Dr. Matteo had helped, but Floyd couldn't stem the idea that she'd taken a couple dozen steps backward recently.

Even before Marcus Slasinsky had reappeared in her life, the situation with Stitts had visibly worn on her.

Floyd's phone started to ring again.

"Dunbar," he said with a frown.

"Let it go to voice mail," Drake instructed.

Floyd slipped his phone back into his pocket.

"All right, it's all done now," Hanna hollered out to them.

Floyd gestured for Drake to exit the room first, but the man insisted that he leave first. He still didn't know much about Drake beyond what Chase had told him in passing, but he knew enough to appreciate that this was a good man.

A man who could be trusted no matter what.

Chase was buttoning up her shirt when they entered the room and Floyd caught a glimpse of a red smear on her collarbone.

"It's sent," Hanna confirmed.

Floyd nodded.

"Let me see it," Drake said.

Hanna, holding Glenn's cell phone close to her chest, raised an eyebrow.

"Let me just see the damn thing, Hanna."

Hanna looked to Chase for confirmation. She just shrugged, completely disinterested.

"Fine, but you keep your pecker in your pants."

As she passed the phone to Drake, Hanna actually winked at Floyd, which caused his face to flush.

What the hell is wrong with this woman?

Drake took the cell phone and slowly backed into the hallway. Floyd watched curiously as the man appeared to pull out his own cell phone as he walked.

"Now what? We wait?" Chase asked, drawing him back.

"All Dunbar had to do was sign the delivery guy out," Hanna stated. "Or something like that, anyway. He's not going to be much longer. We need to decide what we're going do with *him* before the five-oh arrive."

They all looked at Glenn who was still facing the opposite wall.

"If it were up to me? I would take this broomstick and shove it up his—"

Hanna was interrupted by a flash of red and blue lights that filtered in through the busted front door.

"Speak of the devil," Floyd said with a sigh. "Speak of the devil..."

Chapter 53

DRAKE DID HIS BEST to explain the situation without letting Dunbar into the house behind him. If the look on the man's face was any indication, it was clear that he was having a difficult time processing everything.

"So, you're telling me that Glenn Brick is here, only he's dressing up as his aunt now? And you have him tied to a chair?"

"Yes, to the first part, no to the second; I didn't tie anyone up. That was Floyd and the FBI, who have jurisdiction, remember?" Drake tempered his tone. Even though Dunbar wasn't prone to ego trips, he still felt the need to make sure that his words weren't misinterpreted as a challenge.

"Did he say anything? Did he admit to killing those people? Jesus, Drake, you should have called me the second you found him."

Drake shrugged and raised his palms as if to say, it's not my jurisdiction, either.

"He hasn't said much. To be honest, he's off his fucking rocker—after this is all done, I suspect he's going right back to where he came from: Oak Valley."

Dunbar pressed himself onto his toes and peered into the house.

"What about Agent Stitts? Chase's friend? Her sister? Did he say anything about them? Where they're being held? Shit, what about the man's aunt? The one who owns the house?"

Drake had managed to keep a straight face up until this point, but when Dunbar asked these final two questions, he pictured the woman upstairs with her throat slit and his face must have changed.

"Christ, she's in there, isn't she? He killed her—Glenn killed her."

Drake knew better than to lie to the man. He was fine with skirting the truth, glossing over important details, but he didn't want to out and out lie. After all, when—*if*—this was all said and done, he still needed people to have his back. People who were permanent fixtures in New York City and that didn't include, unfortunately, Floyd or Chase.

"She's dead," Drake confirmed. "Glenn slit her throat. Painted her face, all that shit. As for the others, he hasn't said anything—only confirmed that Marcus is the one who's holding them."

"But you guys came up with a plan without me."

Drake nodded.

"Yeah, we came up with something all right. But for it to work, you're gonna have to keep your men at bay. At least for a little while."

When Dunbar looked ready to protest, Drake went ahead and told the man their plan. By the time he was done, Dunbar's eyes were as large as manhole covers.

"You can't be serious, Drake."

"Like I said, not my jurisdiction. It's the FBI's plan and I'm just rolling with it."

"What the fuck are we going to do with Glenn in the meantime? I have to bring him in. Shit, I have to get forensics in here and the ME to deal with the body upstairs."

Drake's eyes narrowed.

"What—what do you expect me to do? Just stand around and wait for a text that may or may not ever come? For how long, Drake?"

Drake pressed his lips together tightly.

He didn't like this part of the plan either and neither did Chase. But this was the best shot they had to find Marcus.

"As long as it takes. We just need you to keep your men away, including that ME."

"What if Marcus thinks this is all just a trick, Drake? What if he doesn't believe that Chase is dead? Then what? We'll have wasted all this time doing nothing."

Drake sighed heavily and looked over his shoulder at Chase who was trying to wipe the horrible makeup off. She caught his stare and Drake immediately looked away.

"There's one more thing I can do to try to push Marcus over the edge. But you're going to have to help me out here and you can't tell anyone—*especially* Chase. Can you do that, Dunbar? Can you trust me?"

Dunbar fidgeted, but eventually, he jammed his hands into his pockets and his shoulders slumped.

"Do I have a choice, Drake? Do I have a choice in any of this?"

Chapter 54

CHASE TAPPED HER FOOT incessantly. Several times she caught Floyd and then Hanna looking over at her, and she'd stop... only to start up again a few seconds later.

"What if he doesn't call?" she asked.

Her voice didn't even sound her own; it was tight and whiny.

"He'll call, he'll call," Floyd reassured her. The problem was, when their eyes met, he would immediately look away.

It had been a full hour since Hanna had sent the image of her to Marcus from Glenn's phone. During that time, Floyd had once again tried to trace the texts, but Chase was doubtful that the results would be any more specific than before: New York City.

Fuck you very much.

In the interim, Hanna was busy working on Glenn. He was an important part of the plan, too; if Marcus wanted to meet, they had to make sure that Glenn was up for the task. If Marcus sniffed something fishy, being as smart as he was, the man would likely be gone before they even knew he'd arrived.

Problem was, Dunbar had put a stop to their previously relied upon persuasion methods. No longer could they hit him with the broomstick. Instead, the man had tried to offer him less tangible rewards for cooperation: a reduced sentence, more rights in Oak Valley, boosted commissary, that sort of thing. But nothing seemed to appeal to Glenn. He was lost.

Broken.

They all were, to lesser or greater degrees.

As this narrative played out, Chase found herself receding deeper and deeper into herself.

She kept picturing Marcus doing horrible things to Stitts, Louisa, and her sister. This last idea was the most haunting. After what Georgina had been through as a child, and the veneer of normalcy that Chase had shattered, she couldn't imagine what it must be like to once again be a captive of a madman.

A madman who only wanted Chase.

Decades ago, Chase had abandoned Georgina, and it had cost her everything. Now, she was once again guilty of her sister's pain.

"Glenn, if you're not going to help us, there's nothing I can—"

"Dunbar, can I talk to you for a second?"

Chase watched Dunbar move away from Glenn and walk over to Drake. The two men made their way into the hallway and turned their backs to her before talking in hushed voices.

She was watching them, trying to make out what they were saying when she saw a shadow move on the porch.

Chase immediately pulled her gun out and walked toward the door.

Upon seeing her expression, Dunbar and Drake stopped talking and followed her gaze.

"Who's there?" she hissed.

Hanna and Floyd started to follow, but Chase gestured for them to stay with Glenn.

Could it be him? Could Marcus have just said fuck it with all the coordinates and times and instead come here himself? Was he that upset with what Glenn had done that he came to seek vengeance?

Chase didn't hold her breath.

Somehow, she got to the door first, passing both Drake and Dunbar in the process. There was indeed a figure on the porch, weaving back and forth as if trying to avoid the most rotted areas. Clutched in one hand was a thick black bag that reminded

Chase of the one that Marcus Slasinsky used to carry while hunting his victims.

In one fluid motion, Chase stepped through the broken front door and reached out with her free hand. She managed to grab an arm and, using their combined momentum, swung the figure up against the wall.

Someone cried out, but Chase silenced this by pressing her gun to the fleshy part under their chin.

"You mother—"

A flashlight suddenly clicked on and two hands pulled Chase backward before she could clear her vision.

For a split second, she saw Marcus Slasinsky's face. She recognized his sallow cheeks, the dull stare, the thinning hair.

But this mirage quickly vanished. It wasn't Marcus Slasinsky but the mousy woman from the morgue.

The ME who had replaced Beckett.

"It's not him, Chase," Drake said.

Chase, overwhelmed by fatigue and anxiety and stress, took some coaxing to lower her gun.

"Who called you?" she demanded, after collecting herself.

The woman was too preoccupied with rubbing her arm where Chase had grabbed and spun her to answer.

"Who called you?" Chase demanded once more.

When the ME just blubbered something incoherent, Chase faced Dunbar.

"You did? You called her? After I told you to keep all of this out of the media?" She was fuming now, and if it weren't for Drake's hand on her forearm, she might have been tempted to raise her weapon again.

"I didn't call anybody," Dunbar replied, holding up his hands defensively.

Chase pulled free of Drake and glared at him next.

"It was you?"

Drake shook his head.

"No. I—"

"It was Officer Kramer," a meek voice answered.

Chase came full circle, her attention returning to Dr. Karen Nordmeyer.

"Who?"

"Officer Kramer. He called me and said there was a body here." The woman's beady little eyes danced about like balsamic vinegar in a pan of hot oil. "He said you asked about Daniela Shipley and Glenn and… I dunno. He-he-he said there was a body here? Jesus, my arm."

Chase, frustrated beyond belief, growled and stormed back inside the house.

Behind her, she heard Dunbar coaxing Dr. Nordmeyer, placating the bitch. She wanted Dunbar to tell her to fuck off, that there was no body, but she also knew that that wouldn't work.

Dr. Nordmeyer would never leave without a thorough inspection of this shithole.

Her phone chimed in her pocket, only it wasn't the familiar sound of a text or message notification.

In her agitated state, it took Chase several seconds to recognize what it was.

After Washington and the whole William Woodley smear campaign, Director Hampton had suggested that she set up a special RSS Feed to notify her whenever her name was mentioned online. That way, they might be able to strong-arm any bloggers who decided to follow an oft-maligned FBI Agent down the rabbit hole.

But this, as far as she could remember, was the first time that the feed had ever pinged. Even with what had happened in

New Mexico and the media coverage that case had garnered, somehow her name had been kept out of it all.

Maybe someone mentioned my name in passing, something to do with one of my older cases. Like Las Vegas... it had to be coming up on a year or so since I stopped Mike Hartman from blowing up T-Mobile Arena.

But even as this thought formulated in her mind, Chase had a sneaking suspicion that she was wrong.

And when she finally calmed down enough to pull out her phone, her worst fears were realized.

It wasn't a random blog post or anything about her past. It was something new, something prominently displayed on the CNN website.

"What the fuck?"

Chase clicked her highlighted name and took one look at the headline photo before the phone slipped from her hand.

Chapter 55

FLOYD'S FIRST THOUGHT AFTER seeing the look on Chase's face, even before she dropped her phone, was that their plan had backfired.

That instead of wanting to meet with Glenn after receiving Chase's picture, Marcus had simply murdered all of his captives.

In fact, this notion was so strong, that Floyd wasn't even the first one to get to Chase even though he was only standing several feet away when her phone pinged.

That honor was bestowed on Hanna.

"Chase? What's wrong? What happened?"

She wrapped her arm around Chase and slowly lowered her into a chair.

"It's me," Chase whispered. "It's me."

Floyd animated and went to his colleague, picking up her dropped phone along the way. The screen was cracked, but the image was still clearly visible. It was Chase, her face white, her lips red, her bare chest pixelated.

The headline said it all: *Prominent FBI Agent Found Murdered.*

"Shit," Floyd swore.

He showed the phone to Hanna first, then to Drake and Dunbar who had come into the kitchen in response to the commotion. Dr. Karen Nordmeyer appeared out of nowhere and tried to get a glimpse of the screen.

"The body's upstairs," Drake barked.

The woman's mousy features contorted, but she eventually scampered off.

"How did they get it? How the fuck did they get the picture?" Chase asked in a breathy whisper.

They...

Floyd looked at the journalist who'd written the article: *Ivan Meitzer.*

He'd never heard of the man.

"Can we stop it? If I call Director Hampton, I'm sure he can do something about," Floyd said desperately.

"It's too late," Chase said. "It's on CNN, for fuck's sake—probably retweeted a thousand times already."

Floyd handed the phone back to Chase and then slumped against the wall.

He wasn't used to this sort of pressure. After all, this had been his plan. Everything from going to the site of Glenn's first murders to setting Chase up to look like she was dead; that was *his* plan.

Drake had helped things along, surely, but it was Floyd behind it all.

And it was all going to shit.

"Wh-wh-what wuh-wuh-we d-d-d-d-d-do?" Floyd asked. His stutter was so powerful that even he had a hard time understanding what he was saying.

"We stick to the plan," Drake said loudly. "This changes nothing."

Chase rocketed to her feet.

"This changes nothing? *Really*?" She was close to snapping; Floyd could see it, as could Hanna, Dunbar, and Drake. It was evident in the way everyone's body tensed. "This changes *everything*, Drake. When Marcus sees this, he's going to kill her—kill *them*. My sister—"

A high-pitch *ping* cut through Chase's angry voice. Everyone in the room suddenly looked at each other, waiting for someone to claim the cell phone notification as their own. But as the seconds ticked by, the air in the room suddenly became heavy.

When a second *ping* came, Floyd immediately chased the sound with his eyes. It had come from the flip phone on the table. He reached for it, but his hand was shaking so badly that Hanna picked it up first.

"Don't—" Dunbar and Drake shouted in unison.

Hanna gave them a look.

"Relax, it's just a phone, not a fucking pipe bomb."

"What does it say?" Chase whispered.

Hanna appeared to read the message several times before turning the small screen around for them all to see.

"It's just a time and an address," she began slowly. "It appears as if someone saw the news article and wants to meet up."

Floyd tried to swallow, but a wad of cotton balls had suddenly materialized in his throat and made this act impossible.

Hanna, on the other hand, seemed unperturbed. In fact, the strange woman actually grinned.

She turned to Glenn who was huffing into the tape that covered his mouth. Then, in a thick Southern accent, Hanna said, "Looks like you best be puttin' on your favorite outfit, sugar, because your debutante ball is about to begin."

Chapter 56

THEY HAD ONE HOUR; they had one hour to get Glenn to comply and make it back out to the streets where he'd first given the box containing Georgina's dress to Rodney Kong.

One hour wasn't much time, but Drake had yet to have a go at the man. He pulled Floyd aside and outlined his plan. Floyd was skeptical, but everything else they'd tried—threats of violence, promises of reduced sentences—had fallen on deaf ears.

"Worth a shot," Floyd said.

Drake's upper lip twitched.

"Good. I want you to take everyone else outside, then join me back in here. Think you can do that?"

Floyd nodded.

He turned to Dunbar, Chase, and Hanna and relayed Drake's message. He expected Dunbar to complain, to resist, but the man had completely given in now. He actually helped to get Chase to leave the room, even though she was heavily opposed to the idea.

That left only Dr. Nordmeyer upstairs doing whatever the hell she was doing with Daniela Shipley's corpse—but she didn't count.

When they were finally alone, Floyd took up residence near the back wall and watched Drake work.

"He used you, Glenn or Glenda, or whatever the hell you want to be called. Doesn't really matter what name you use, because Marcus Slasinsky used you," Drake began in a monotone voice. With every word, Glenn's smile grew. Drake was undeterred. "Let me ask you something, Glenn: why did you kill those guards at Oak Valley? Why did you kill the guy in the field?"

"They were mocking me, making fun of me," the man replied. Drake grabbed Glenn's chin in his hand and held it firm, preventing him from looking away.

Floyd watched this interaction curiously. This was the most open that Glenn had been with any of them.

"Really? Those two guards mocked you? Glenn—Glenn, c'mon. I was there, remember? I was a patient at Oak Valley, and I know those guards. They were strict but fair. One thing they never did was mock anyone."

Floyd had no idea if this was true, if he really knew the dead orderlies, but it struck a chord with Glenn and he tried to break free of Drake's hold.

He failed.

"They all made fun of me. I saw it—it was the way they looked at me."

"And the man in the field?"

Glenn sneered.

"They were picking on somebody and they needed to pay. That's what Auntie Shipley always said: if you get picked on, make them pay. If they don't stop, make them stop."

Drake nodded slowly.

"So, your aunt told you to make people who picked on you, tried to manipulate you, pay, am I right?"

Glenn's lips twitched.

"Yeah. That's what she told me." His voice suddenly changed into the hoarse whisper that Floyd had heard when he'd first come to the door. "Stop being such a pushover; stick up for yourself."

"That's why you killed her, right? That's why you killed your aunt? Because she picked on you?"

"She deserved it," Glenn replied instantly.

"Yeah, I bet she did."

Drake looked at Floyd, and it took him a moment to realize that he was expecting some sort of affirmation.

Floyd gave it to him.

"Anybody who castrates a young boy deserves what they get," he said without a stutter.

Drake turned back to Glenn.

"See? We agree with you."

Floyd didn't like where this was going. Glenn had gone from psychotic to manic to now angry. Sure, he was injured—his shoulder was more than likely separated—but the chair wouldn't hold forever.

Still, for now, it appeared as if Drake knew what he was doing.

"Let me ask you something else, Glenn: what's your obsession with butterflies?"

The anger in Glenn's face became confusion.

"Butterflies?"

"Yeah, butterflies; you drew butterflies on your victims' chests. You didn't do that in the high school, though, with your first two victims. Only these most recent murders. The people you killed *after* speaking to Marcus Slasinsky at Oak Valley. So, I'm going to just go ahead and assume that these butterflies *weren't* your idea."

"They were," Glenn said quickly. "They were my idea."

Drake sighed and leaned away from the man.

"Really, Glenn? Why butterflies, then?"

"Because… because… because I fucking like them, that's why!"

Now Drake rose to his feet and crossed his arms over his chest.

"I don't think so, Glenn. I don't think you give a shit about butterflies. But you know what? There's one man who does:

Marcus Slasinsky. And you know what else I think? I think Marcus was making fun of you."

"Making fun of me? He got me out."

Drake gestured to the room around them.

"Did he, though? I mean, you're not really free, are you? You being here, strapped to this chair, was all part of Marcus' plan. But those butterflies, you know what those butterflies are?"

"Insects—what the fuck is your point? I know what butterflies are, everybody knows what butterflies are."

"Insects, sure. But they're more than that. They represent a transformation. You see, butterflies are just caterpillars that underwent a majestic change."

Floyd couldn't help but smirk. Drake might claim that he was just the muscle, but the man also had a brain.

"So what?" Glenn snapped. "What does that matter? What do I care?"

He was like a petulant child, and because of what his aunt had done to him, he hadn't undergone a majestic transformation of his own.

Which was exactly the point that Drake was trying to make. But instead of beating this into the man, Drake just leaned back and continued to stare.

Floyd was more than impressed now. He'd learned from Stitts that ideas and revelations held far more meaning and impact if you came to them on your own, rather than being force-fed. There was immense value in learning something by yourself rather than being explicitly told by a teacher or parent.

And when that happened, no matter how much it was implied or suggested, the singular spark of that idea rooted itself in your brain like some sort of parasite.

Or a worm.

Better yet, a caterpillar.

"So what?" Glenn shouted now. He tried to break free of his bindings, but they held. This was anger, surely, but it wasn't manic rage like before. This was the anger of realization. "So what? I like butterflies! I like butterflies!"

Without another word, Drake walked over to Floyd and put his arm around his shoulder. Then he guided them out onto the porch where the others were waiting.

Behind them, Glenn continued to shout and struggle.

Chase opened her mouth to say something, but Drake brought a finger to his lips. After a few minutes, Glenn's antics started to die down.

Soon after, soft sobs could be heard from the kitchen.

"I think he's ready," Drake said. "I think he's going to help us now."

Chapter 57

CHASE HAD NO IDEA what Drake had said to Glenn, but it did appear as if the man was now open to the idea of getting back at Marcus Slasinsky.

But still, she wasn't taking any chances.

"Anyone have that tape?" she asked the group.

Hanna produced a roll of duct tape and handed it to her. Chase walked over to Glenn, ignored his strange look, and tore off a piece just longer than his mouth. As soon as he saw her hand coming toward his face, Glenn tried to look away, but Dunbar was there and held his head firmly.

She pressed the tape tightly to his lips, smoothing the corners down as much as possible.

"So, you like to paint your victims' faces, do you?" she said just loud enough for Glenn and maybe Dunbar to hear.

With Dunbar still holding the man's head, Chase removed the red lipstick that had once been used to mark her own lips and drew an ugly set over the top of the tape. Then she turned to Hanna and gestured towards the rest of the makeup lying on the kitchen table.

"Want to give me a hand here? We need to fix him up a bit, get him looking like Glenda and not Glenn."

Hanna didn't hesitate. In fact, she almost seemed excited at the prospect.

Ten minutes later, Glenda had arrived.

"That's pretty close to how he looked when we got here," Floyd offered. "I think."

Glenn tried to say something, but with his mouth covered in tape that had since been painted over with makeup, all he managed was an incoherent muffled sound.

Chase was happy to see that the tape held. She took a step back and indicated for Floyd to remove the ropes from the man's wrists and ankles. He did, then hoisted Glenda to his feet. For a moment, it looked like Glenda might try to make a run for the back door, but Drake smoothly moved to block his path.

Floyd must have noticed this too, as he quickly slapped a set of handcuffs on her.

"I'll take them off once we get there," Floyd promised.

"Everyone ready? Everyone know what their jobs are?" Chase asked.

Every single person in the room acknowledged that they did.

"Then let's go. Let's catch this asshole and get my friends and family back."

Chapter 58

IT WASN'T DIFFICULT FOR Drake and Chase to find the street worker who they'd spoken to earlier in the night. And after Chase apologized for her outburst, Heather agreed to help them again.

For a fee, of course.

Chase backed down an alleyway and when she was sure that they were alone, Heather approached.

"You're sure this is… legal?" Heather asked when she saw Glenda handcuffed in the backseat. "How does this—I don't get how this has anything to do with your missing dress."

Chase and Drake pulled Glenda out of the car and gave her a once over.

She was sweating, and her makeup had started to run, but the lighting was poor, and Chase deemed it a good enough disguise in a pinch.

"It's a long story," she replied.

"Look, I don't know if I want to be getting involved in—"

Chase flashed her FBI badge quickly so that the woman could see the insignia and the logo, but not long enough for her to read the name.

"Jesus, you're a Fed?"

Sensing that this had made the woman more rather than less nervous, Chase placated her with a simple gesture.

"I already paid you, and you agreed to help. If you run now…"

Heather swallowed hard, realizing that she was in a bind.

"What do you want me to do?" she asked at last.

"Keep her in the shadows. When a specific client comes, I want you to make sure that he sees her. Not up close, just enough to recognize who it is. Shouldn't be that hard given how tall she is."

"Specific client? How am I going to know *which* client?"

"You'll know."

"But how? I mean—"

"You'll know," Chase repeated sternly. Then she roughly spun Glenda around.

"The rules are different for you, big girl. You run and I'll fucking hunt you down—I'll make what your aunt did to you feel like summer camp."

Glenda huffed into the tape but relaxed when Chase finally uncuffed her.

"She's your responsibility now," Chase said to Heather.

The prostitute nodded, but it was clear that she was scared.

Chase produced yet another hundred-dollar bill from her pocket and held it out. But when Heather reached for it, she pulled back.

"*After*. Just be calm, be normal."

With that, Chase and Drake watched Heather awkwardly guide Glenda back out to the street. True to their plan, she made sure that the much taller woman stayed out of sight.

"All right, Chase, I'm going to walk down to the end of the street and wait there. No matter what happens, though, you have to stay in your car until we have Marcus in cuffs. You can have the first crack at him, but you have to stay in the car. Promise me that."

Chase looked him directly in the eyes.

"I promise."

Drake wasn't convinced, but they were out of time; their hour was nearly up. He was about to walk away when she reached for his arm and pulled him back.

"Thank you," she said softly. "Thank you, Drake."

Drake just stared at her, confused by the sudden outburst of emotion.

"Don't thank—"

Before he could get the words out, Chase pulled him down and kissed him full on the lips.

Drake knew that this was a bad idea on many levels; he knew that she was acting irrationally, that her emotions were heightened and that she wasn't thinking straight. He also had his girlfriend and child to think about.

But he couldn't stop it. He couldn't stop it because Chase had a strange hold on him, a hold that ran deep.

Drake kissed her back.

Eventually, it was Chase who peeled her lips from his.

"It was me who called Officer Kramer to let him know that there was a body in Daniela Shipley's house," he blurted. "I was also the one who sent your picture to a contact I have in the media."

Chase's face seemed to cave inward like a thumb pushed into the side of a warm candle.

"What? Why?"

"He wasn't going to fall for it, Chase. Marcus… he wouldn't believe that you were dead unless your face was plastered all over the news. I'm sorry, but I had to do it."

This wasn't the time for such an admission, but Drake seemed to have lost all control over his mouth and emotions.

"You… you lied to me."

Drake started to back away.

"I'm sorry, Chase. I just did what I had to do to get your friends back. Trust me, if I thought there was any other way…" Chase's eyes started to water. "Please, just stay in your car, Chase; no matter what, stay in your car."

Worried that he might lose his resolve, Drake flipped the hood over his head and hustled down the street, not even bothering to cast a glance at Heather or Glenda.

When he made it to his post about a half-block away, he turned back.

Chase was no longer in the alleyway, but he couldn't see her in her dark car, either. He just hoped that she was in there, that she would listen to him, that she would forgive him, one day.

With a sigh, he pulled the walkie-talkie out of the center pocket of his sweatshirt and brought it to his lips.

"Everyone in position?" he asked softly.

Hanna, Dunbar, and Floyd replied in succession that they were ready. Drake waited for a ten count for Chase to chime in but then gave up.

If she'd taken off, if she'd done something stupid, there was no way for him to intervene now. They still had to find Stitts and Louisa and Georgina.

The rest could wait.

"Then shut down communication," Drake said, turning off his own walkie.

Tucking out of sight, Drake leaned back and waited. In his mind, he counted down the seconds until he was positive that an hour had passed since Marcus had sent the message with the coordinates where Glenn should meet him.

Nothing changed. Sure, people came and went—Johns and prostitutes—and several cars slowed to the spot where Drake could just barely make out Glenda and Heather's outlines, but there was no sign of Marcus.

Every once in a while, Drake allowed his eyes to drift across the street at the car that sat idling with its lights off.

Hanna was seated behind the wheel, he knew. Not only that, but further down, in the opposite direction, Floyd and Dunbar sat waiting in his unmarked car.

C'mon you motherfucker—show up.

Drake tried to stay calm, tried to resist the urge to reach out to the others to see if they'd noticed anything suspicious.

Just wait.

His patience paid off.

Just as his hand closed on the walkie inside his pocket, he saw a black car slowly approach the area where Heather and Glenda stood. It didn't stand out in any discernible way… except for the fact that he'd already seen it once before.

Roughly five minutes ago, Drake had seen the car drive by, slow, then take off. He suspected that this wasn't completely out of the ordinary for a first time John, but now that it had returned a second time…

Go now, he silently urged. *Heather, push Glenda into the light. Do it now!*

But when there was no movement from the shadows, Drake cursed out loud.

We're going to miss him… Marcus isn't going to see Glenn and he's going to—

Just then, a tall, lanky woman with heavy makeup on her face stepped onto the sidewalk.

It was Glenda, and Drake's adrenaline surged.

As soon as he rolls down the window and I see his face, it's over, Drake thought. *We'll have him boxed in in minutes. Just show your face, Marcus. Show your goddamn face.*

But the window didn't roll down. Instead, the passenger door started to open.

"What the hell?"

By the time Drake saw the gagged and bound body being shoved onto the sidewalk, it was too late.

He pulled his walkie-talkie free from his pocket and switched it on, all the while starting to move toward Glenda.

"Stay in the car, Chase," he hushed as loud as he dared. "Stay in the car."

The body flopped onto the sidewalk with a sickening thud. Even though he was still a half-block away, Drake thought he recognized the person. Chase must have too because she was suddenly running from the alleyway toward the road.

"No, Chase! *No!*"

Drake dropped the walkie-talkie and started to sprint.

"No!"

The door to the black car slammed shut and its tires squealed like a thousand New York City rats all vying for the same morsel of cheese.

Chapter 59

HANNA COULD SEE THE black car, but she couldn't tell what was happening on the other side of it. When she saw Drake and Chase running down the sidewalk toward one another, however, she knew that this was it.

When she heard the tires of the black car scream, Hanna acted.

She flicked on her headlights and slammed her foot against the accelerator. Her VW shot forward with incredible speed, so much speed, in fact, that she was pinned against the back of her seat. She adjusted the steering wheel slightly, making sure that the front of her one-ton torpedo was aimed at the ass-end of what could only be Marcus Slasinsky's car.

Her aim *would* have been perfect. Even though the black car shot forward, her VW would have collided with the rear bumper, sending them both into a jarring, yet controlled spin.

But in the darkness of night, Hanna didn't see the pothole halfway between her car and Marcus Slasinsky's. Her left tire hit it hard enough to tear a gaping hole and launch Hanna into the air. She cried out, no easy feat considering how clenched her jaw was, and her right hand yanked the steering wheel down.

The car nearly flipped over when it came crashing back to the pavement. On its second bounce, it still somehow managed to strike the back of the black car—only it didn't make contact with the side of the bumper as she'd planned, but directly behind it.

Almost like an encouraging shove.

Not that Hanna saw any of this; she'd already been rendered unconscious.

Chapter 60

"Stitts! *Stitts!*" Chase screamed. She wrapped her arms around her partner and flipped him onto his back. "Stitts!"

He was alive—Stitts was alive and Chase had never been so happy to see anybody in her entire life. She raked her nails across the tape that covered his mouth and yanked it off.

Stitts' eyes went wide, and he sucked in a huge, shuddering breath. By the way he was blinking and staring not at Chase but *through* her, it was clear that he had no idea where he was.

And perhaps even *who* he was.

Chase reached out and grabbed his face, trying to get the man to focus on her.

"Stitts, it's me! it's Chase!"

His eyelids fluttered.

"Chase?"

"Yes," she sobbed. Tears fell from her cheeks and landed on Stitts' flushed face. "Yeah, it's me. Thank God, you're okay."

Stitts was looking at her now and crying, too. Chase leaned down and hugged him tightly, despite his protests. She was rambling, telling Stitts that she missed him and loved him.

A horrific crunch followed by the sound of twisting metal nearly made Chase drop Stitts back to the sidewalk. She looked up in time to see a Volkswagen rock on its chassis. Thinking that it would roll on top of them, she cradled Stitts' head in her arms, as if that would protect him.

The front tires smashed into the curb, causing the vehicle to bounce, but stopping its imminent roll.

One glimpse of the dark head of hair smashing into the driver's side airbag and everything flooded back.

Marcus! Marcus had thrown Stitts from the car!

The black car was propelled forward by the VW and fishtailed wildly. It appeared at first as if it was going to spin out, but the driver somehow managed to right it moments before that happened. The violent adjustments caused a hubcap to shoot off and roll down the street like metallic tumbleweed, but the car continued to pick up speed.

"No!" she screamed, images of Louisa and Georgina flashing in her mind. "No!"

As smoke and burning rubber filled her lungs, Chase turned back to Stitts and shook him gently.

"Where is she, Stitts? Where's my sister? Where is he keeping her?"

Stitts appeared confused, and she jostled him harder.

"Where is she?"

The man's lips moved but she couldn't hear any sound.

"What?"

Somewhere nearby Drake shouted, and Chase leaned in close to Stitts' mouth to make out the words.

"The Butterfly Gardens," her partner whispered.

Chase immediately lowered him to the ground and then rose to her feet.

Drake was coming at her full steam, and she knew she had to get away before he grabbed her.

"Look after him," she yelled as she started to run toward her car in the alley. "Please, Drake! Look after him!"

"Chase! Stop! *Stop!*"

But Chase didn't stop. Instead, she put all of the hours and hours she'd spent running, trying desperately to get away from her problems, to good use by finally running *toward* something.

Toward her sister and her friend, and the man who'd taken them from her.

Chapter 61

The second Floyd heard Drake's voice over the radio, when he heard his friend shouting for Chase to stay in the car, he knew that something had gone terribly wrong.

"Drive!" he yelled to Dunbar. "Drive! Drive! *Drive!*"

Dunbar immediately shifted his unmarked cruiser into drive and flicked on the cherry that sat on the dash. The vehicle leaped forward, quickly closing the distance between them and the black car.

Floyd was fumbling with his gun, trying to get it out of the holster while seated when he heard a resonant thump.

He looked up just as Hanna's car went airborne, then came crashing back down again.

"Shit!"

The black car that Hanna had grazed started to spin and for a brief second, it looked as if they were heading for a head-on collision. But the driver—*Marcus, it had to be Marcus*—went with the rotation and at the last moment, sped up a narrow alleyway.

Dunbar gripped the steering wheel as if he was trying to wring water out of it.

"Hang on," he grumbled.

Floyd was adjusting his ass in the seat when he spotted two people on the sidewalk. One was Chase, while the other was—

"Stitts!" he gasped.

"What?"

"Stitts! It's Stitts!" Floyd cried, pointing at the man with the messy hair and soiled clothing lying on the ground.

When it didn't appear as if Dunbar was going to call off the chase, Floyd reached for the wheel.

"What the fuck are you doing?"

"Go to them! Go to them!"

Dunbar swatted his hand away, but Floyd didn't stop trying to grab the steering wheel.

He wasn't thinking rationally—at that moment, Floyd didn't give a shit about catching Marcus Slasinsky. All he cared about was Chase and Stitts. The two people who had taken a chance on him when everyone else in the world had passed him off as being slow, useless.

And now they needed his help.

Dunbar must have realized that Floyd wasn't going to stop and if they continued in this way—with Floyd desperately trying to steer the car—they were equally as likely to run Chase over as they were to follow Marcus. The detective gave up and pulled the cruiser to a screeching halt but inches from Hanna's smoking car.

Floyd immediately jumped out, but Chase was on the move. She was sprinting back toward the alley.

"Chase!" he yelled. But his voice was swallowed by Drake's who was also shouting her name.

Floyd debated going after her, but a split-second triage pushed him toward Stitts instead. Drake beat him there, but Floyd shoved the much bigger man out of the way.

"Stitts, you okay? Tell me you're okay!"

"He's alive," Drake huffed in his ear. "Stitts is alive."

"What the fuck happened?" Dunbar yelled.

"Stitts," was the only word that Floyd could say. He leaned down and hugged his friend, but when Stitts didn't return the gesture, he looked to Dunbar. "Call an ambulance!"

Dunbar was one step ahead of him; he was already on his radio asking for an EMT.

Out of the corner of his eye, Floyd saw Drake slowly slinking toward the crowd of prostitutes and other onlookers who had begun to form around them.

"Drake, where are you going?" Floyd demanded, still cradling Stitts' head in his arms.

But the man's destination was suddenly clear: Dunbar's still running unmarked cruiser.

Chapter 62

EVEN THOUGH IT HAD been close to two years since Chase had been to the Butterfly Gardens, which had long since been condemned, she didn't need directions. The location of the large, once impressive geodesic dome was etched in her memory, in a way that only traumatic events could imprint.

Ones that hadn't been intentionally erased or confounded via electroshock therapy or the consumption of illicit substances, that is.

She drove as fast as she dared, speeding through stop signs, blowing through red lights, and cutting off anybody who got in her way.

Her goal was singular: to find Georgina.

Finding Georgina would put an end to all of her problems, she knew. Finding Georgina would alleviate the guilt that had wracked her for decades.

Finding Georgina would be a way to right all of the wrongs that she'd done over the years, repair relationships with all the people that she'd hurt, all of the people that she'd lied to.

Chase weaved around the bent and rusted gate and passed several placards indicating that the space was destined to become high-rise apartments in the years to come.

The vegetation growing through fissures in the asphalt was so thick in places that her tires lost traction. But eventually, she made it to the geodesic dome that was the Butterfly Gardens. Unlike two years ago when all of the panes of glass had been smashed, they had been replaced with plywood to keep out rain, vagrants, and wildlife.

Chase's BMW bumped the curb and she got out without even bothering to turn it off.

The thick metal doors that marked the entrance appeared bound by a chain, but on closer inspection, Chase realized that there was no lock present. She tore the chain away and tossed it aside.

Chase pulled her gun out of the holster and then stepped inside the Butterfly Gardens.

She was immediately met with a vegetal smell that was so thick that it was difficult to draw a full breath. Yet, Chase pressed onward. After but a handful of steps, the heavy entrance doors swung closed, bathing her in darkness. Still breathing shallowly through her mouth, Chase laid her flashlight on top of the barrel of her pistol and flicked it on.

Chernobyl.

It was the first word that came to mind. Not the idea of Chernobyl immediately following the disaster, but years later when life had returned without human intervention.

The weeds and shoots were waist high in places and with every step, Chase stirred up dozens of airborne insects, thankfully, none of which were butterflies. Even with all these plants colluding to try and slow her progress, Chase kept on plowing through, making her way toward the center of the dome.

"Marcus?" a female voice asked.

All the blood left Chase's limbs.

"Marcus?"

The tears that streamed down her face after finding Stitts alive were but a trickle compared to the deluge that she experienced now.

Even though she couldn't feel her legs, Chase somehow continued to move forward.

This numbness reminded her of the first time she'd used heroin.

I can make you forget, Tyler Tisdale had promised her. And for a time, he had.

Chase took in a full breath, swallowing dozens of spores, then raised her flashlight.

And that's when she saw her.

Standing on the makeshift stage wearing jeans and a black T-shirt, her hair cropped close to her scalp, was her sister, Georgina Adams.

But there was something wrong with the scene. Something off.

Georgina wasn't bound and gagged as Louisa and Stitts had been but standing upright. She even seemed to have her hands in her pockets.

This… this can't be right. She just escaped—after Marcus took off with Stitts, she broke free but didn't know where to go.

Movement in front of her sister drew Chase's gaze.

Louisa sat slumped in a chair, her hair wet and stringy, her face slick with perspiration.

Why didn't she untie Louisa?

"Marcus?" Georgina asked again, shielding her eyes with the blade of her hand as she stared into Chase's bright flashlight.

"Georgina?"

The thin woman tucked her chin to her chest and upon seeing Chase, her face split into a sneer.

"You."

"Yeah—Georgina, it's me, it's Chase. Your sister."

But Georgina's expression didn't change. She did, however, crouch down, and lean in close to Louisa's thick throat.

"You come any closer and I'll kill her."

Chase blinked, thinking that not only had she misheard, but that she wasn't actually seeing her sister forcing something sharp against her friend's flesh.

"Georgina... Marcus is gone—he's gone. He had you, he took you, but now he's gone. You're free."

Georgina laughed.

"Free! Ha! You silly bitch; Marcus never took me."

It felt like a cinder block had been dropped on Chase's chest.

"Georgina, please—"

"Take another step, and I'll kill your friend," Georgina warned again.

To prove that she was serious, she pressed the knife or scalpel or whatever it was deep enough to send a rivulet of blood cascading down Louisa's collarbone.

The woman barely flinched.

"I don't... I don't understand."

The gun in Chase's hand suddenly felt as if it weighed a thousand pounds. She dropped it into the vegetation, without a second thought.

"Georgina—"

"My name's not Georgina," the woman hissed, "it's Riley—Riley Jalston. You took everything from me, Chase, and today I'm going to make you pay."

Chapter 63

THE RADIO EMBEDDED IN the dash of Dunbar's unmarked police cruiser was alive with voices, each one calling for a different emergency service.

Drake paid nearly as little attention to them as he did Floyd and Dunbar who were both shouting at him as he pulled away from the curb.

Stitts was alive, which meant that there was a high probability that Louisa and Georgina were also amongst the living.

And then there was Chase, doing what Chase did: taking off without telling anybody where she was going or what her plan was.

The woman believed that she had to take on everything in this world on her own, that, somehow, humanity's plight was solely her responsibility to rectify.

Drake was determined to prove her wrong.

With the cherry still flashing, he turned down the alley that Marcus' car had fled down moments before. It was so narrow that when he reached the first intersection, there was only one way that he *could* turn. When he was put to a decision moments later, he rolled down the window and inhaled deeply. The trail of burning rubber was the only guide he needed.

After five minutes of snaking down narrow street after narrow street, Drake finally caught sight of the black sedan with the crumpled rear bumper, slowing before making a hard right onto a main road.

Drake gunned it.

He'd let Marcus Slasinsky get away once before with only superficial injuries; he wasn't about to let that happen again. But just before he got close enough to initiate the PIT maneuver, Drake suddenly changed his mind.

Georgina was still out there...

With Stitts and Louisa, Drake had been worried about their safety, about what Marcus might do to them in order to claim his ultimate prize: Chase.

When it came to Georgina, however, it was Chase herself for whom Drake feared.

His ex-partner still believed that Georgina was a victim, a cog in Marcus' master plan, and while this might be true in the philosophical sense, Chase was the one who was in imminent danger. If she was making her way toward Georgina, if Stitts had managed to communicate where they were being held as he lay on the sidewalk, then she was probably walking into an ambush.

Drake also knew that Chase, despite being as hardened as she was, would never hurt her sister, her family.

Unlike him.

People say that family is the most important thing in this world, that the blood bond you share is powerful, unbreakable, but the reality is that you don't get to pick who you are related to.

It came down to simple luck of the draw.

You did, however, select your friends, the people you spend time with, those who mean the most to you.

And once you pick your circle of friends, no matter how small, no matter how trying, you had to remain loyal.

You had to protect them from others, from you, and sometimes even from themselves.

Drake reached up and shut off the flashing light then fell back a few dozen yards.

He surmised that Marcus must have seen Chase take off. Drake figured that the man's obsession was so great that he would be compelled to head back to his captives in order to lure Chase in.

Marcus was obsessed, he was manic, suffered from schizoid split-personality disorder, and he would do anything to have Chase.

Even if it meant that his plan was thrown to the wind.

When the black car started to obey street signs and slowed down to near the speed limit, Drake fell back even further, convinced that Marcus thought he was in the clear.

The incessant squawking of the police scanner was starting to annoy him, so Drake turned it off. As Marcus started to head away from the city, Drake suddenly became aware that even though the landscape had changed over the intervening years—more new developments had sprouted on either side of the municipal highway—he recognized where they were headed.

"Idiot," he grumbled.

The answer was right there in front of them all along; shit, Floyd had even told them where Marcus was keeping his victims, if not in so many words.

If Glenn Brick was drawn to the place that held the most meaning to him, the house that inspired a visceral emotional reaction deep inside his soul, then Marcus, smart as he was, would likely be coerced by this same inclination.

It was Drake who was the stupid one, not Marcus. He even considered the possibility that the whole Oak Valley incident, tracking Glenn Brick, and chasing down Georgina's dress might not have been part of Marcus' original plan. It might have simply been the man's response to them taking too long to find him.

Marcus had probably been waiting for them at this location since it all began.

The place that held a special spot in his heart.

The place where Chase had gotten away.

Drake's eyes lifted to an old green road sign. The weather had stripped away nearly all of its reflective qualities, and even though he could make out but a handful of letters, Drake knew exactly what the sign said: *Butterfly Gardens.*

And that, he had no doubt, was where Marcus was headed.

Chapter 64

"**You took everything from** me," Georgina Adams repeated. She was still crouched behind Louisa, even though Chase only held a flashlight in her hands now.

Despite her sister's insistence to remain where she was, Chase slowly strode forward.

"I'm sorry," Chase said. "I was a little girl, not much older than you, and I didn't know what I was doing."

Georgina's brow furrowed

"What are you talking about?"

"We were both little girls, so young… and it was hot down there. I was… I was lost, Georgie. I saw Louisa get out and she tossed me the plate she used to dig under the bars. I didn't even know you were there—I didn't know anything. All I wanted to do is get *out*, get back to mom and dad. I'm so, so sorry."

"What the fuck are you talking about?" Georgina spat, her anger mounting.

Chase wiped tears from her face and continued forward.

"I want to tell you that I was trying to escape so that I could get help, get someone to come back for you, but I won't lie anymore. I left because I was scared… I was just a scared little girl who didn't know *anything*. Georgina, I would do anything now to have switched places with you."

Georgina's hands were trembling ever so slightly, which caused more blood to spill into the hollow of Louisa's throat.

"I told you before," she said through clenched teeth. "My name is Riley, and I don't know who you are."

Chase shook her head.

"Yes, you do, Georgina—you're my sister. I left you that day beneath the house, behind bars. I left you alone in that horrible place."

"You *left* me? You *came* for me. You killed my dad, you killed Tim Jalston—I saw you stab him. And if that wasn't enough, then you took my sisters and Brian away from me. You left me with *nothing*."

Chase shook her head slowly from side to side.

"They weren't your family, Georgina. *I* am your family. Those people… Tim and Brian Jalston? They kidnapped you. They took both of us, but I got away. Then they raped you. Raped your mind and your body. And the people you call your sisters? They were just other girls like you who were taken from their families. Tim and Brian Jalston were never your family, Georgina. *I* am."

A pained expression suddenly appeared on Georgina's face.

"No," she whispered.

Chase experienced her sister's anguish as if it were her own; she knew firsthand how it felt to have two different memories colliding in your brain, the confusion of not being able to discern fantasy from reality.

It was what had driven Chase to heroin in the first place.

"You're lying," Georgina said, but her voice wasn't as strong as it had been moments ago. "You're trying to trick me… Brian warned me that this might happen. I don't remember you. I don't *know* you."

Chase took another step forward. She was right at the lip of the stage now, only a dozen feet from her sister and Louisa.

"They're the ones who tricked you, Georgie. I know how confusing this must be. Trust me, I know, but I can help you. I'll spend every day with you, every single day, trying to get you to remember. You're a victim here—a victim to Brian and Tim and to Marcus. And you need help. I—I want to be the one to help you."

Georgina pulled the knife away from Louisa's throat. As Chase stepped up onto the stage, she could see tears welling in her sister's eyes.

"I don't know who I am," Georgina whispered. "I have nobody... you took everything from me."

"No, no, that's not true, Georgie," Chase said as she closed even more ground. "You have me. And you have a daughter. You have a beautiful daughter who needs you."

Chase stopped and extended her hand to her sister.

"I'm Riley," Georgina repeated, nearly sobbing now. "My name's Riley Jalston."

Georgina slowly rose to her feet and the knife she'd been holding slipped from her hand.

Her entire body was shaking.

"No, it's not," Chase said softly. "Your name is Georgina Adams; my name is Chase Adams and your father's name was Kevin Adams. Your mother was Kerry Adams."

Georgina slowly raised her hand and stared at it as if it belonged to someone else.

Then she stared directly into Chase's eyes.

"Was?"

Chase fought back tears. She debated lying to Georgie, telling her that her dad hadn't committed suicide, that he was alive and well, and that their mother wasn't demented and in a home.

But she couldn't do that. Lying was what had fucked them both up in the first place.

"You have me, Georgie. We have each other."

For a moment, there was an impasse, but then Georgina extended her hand toward Chase's. The second their fingers touched, images flooded Chase's mind, images from their childhood before all this happened, before they were taken.

Chase relived their happy life in Franklin, Tennessee, riding their bikes around the neighborhood, enjoying barbecue cookouts on their street, and bouncing on a trampoline in their backyard.

Time sped forward, and she saw Georgina writing on a giant stone in the woods, putting hearts around three individual letters: *K*, *K*, and *C*.

She saw her sister surrounded by women in white dresses, cheering her on. She saw Georgina's sweaty face, heard her grunts, her screams, as she gave birth to her child.

"Chase?" Georgina whispered.

Chase's eyes snapped open.

The woman before her wasn't in her early thirties, but much, much younger. A series of freckles dotted her slightly-upturned nose, and her green eyes were wide and wet.

Blue snow cone syrup staining her heart-shaped lips.

"I remember, Chase. I remember—"

The sound of three distinct gunshots cut Georgina off mid-sentence, and Chase screamed.

Chapter 65

FOR THE MOST PART, serial killers are predictable animals. They have a specific victim type, a particular MO, and a familiar ritual they perform both before and after their kills.

But they are rarely stagnant beings. Over time, their methodology changes, it evolves, usually becoming more and more sadistic in a pathetic attempt to recreate the dopamine dump of their first kill.

This was also true of Marcus Slasinsky, heightened intelligence or not. After all, no matter how much we try to deny our impulses, humans are often beholden to our lizard brains, acting and reacting in ways that evolution programmed us to react in centuries earlier.

At their core, serial killers were psychopaths, and when pushed, their actions became unpredictable.

For Marcus Slasinsky, his kills had all been personal. After his abusive father abandoned him, he was left with a severely depressed mother who not only didn't look after him but cried all the time. Marcus, delirious and confused from lack of sleep, made her stop the only way he knew how: he slit his mother's wrists. Perhaps he was ashamed of what he'd done, or maybe he was trying to avoid the consequences of his actions. Either way, Marcus lived with his mother's corpse for weeks. When neighbors complained of the smell, he opened the windows.

That's when the insects came, particularly Monarchs, and took up residence inside Martha Slasinsky's decomposing corpse.

Eventually, the cops were called, and Marcus was taken away and subjected to treatment. Given that he was a minor, all of his records were supposed to be sealed, but somehow his colleagues at school heard about what he'd done and started to torment him for it.

Everything culminated here, at the Butterfly Gardens. The kids tricked him, mocked him, and eventually forced him into a field of butterflies.

Marcus' mind broke.

Years later, after adopting a new identity as Dr. Mark Kruk, something happened, and Marcus was triggered. The man sought out the four kids—now adults—who had caused him so much pain years ago.

He'd killed them one by one by injecting a slurry of butterfly carcasses into their bloodstream.

Chase had been the outlier; she was the one heading up the investigation into what the media had dubbed the Butterfly Killer and Marcus had fixated on her.

In his mind, Chase *was* his mother, she was the physical embodiment of Martha Slasinsky, and in order to finish his ritualistic revenge, he had to kill her all over again.

Over time, had he been successful in this quest, Drake had no doubt that the cycle would have repeated itself. Marcus would have found four new people who had tormented him, or others like him, and murdered them, as well.

And yet, Drake never expected Marcus to be acting the way he was now: desperate, irrational, unpredictable.

"Stop! Marcus, *stop!*"

The man had leaped from the black sedan and was now heading toward the doors of the Butterfly Gardens. Drake braced himself on the hood of his car and took aim with his gun, but the man darted inside before he could squeeze off a shot.

"Fuck."

Drake started after him, running as fast as he could, but slowed when he saw a second car parked in front of Marcus'.

The door hung open and the interior was empty, save a cell phone lying on the passenger seat.

Chase's cell phone.

Drake cursed again, as his fears were borne out: Stitts *had* told her where Marcus had been keeping them and he feared that she had just walked into a trap.

Drake continued toward the doors and eventually threw them wide and stepped into the Gardens.

"Marcus!" he yelled again.

The overgrown vegetation was high in places, but it was easier going for Drake than Marcus, as he stayed to the path that the man or Chase had already crushed and flattened.

After about twenty large strides, Drake saw him: Marcus Slasinsky stood adroitly, his hands out in front of him not thirty feet from the stage.

If the man had a history of violence with guns or even a hint of such base crimes, Drake wouldn't have hesitated. But Marcus was a personal killer, one who liked to see the look in his victims' eyes before they passed. He wanted those he killed to know that it was he who had taken their life.

Guns were impersonal, imprecise, unsophisticated.

But Marcus had been pushed, his plan derailed. And, more importantly, the serial killer wasn't looking for another victim—not directly, anyway.

He was looking for revenge, but not on an individual person; he was looking for retribution on the world for all of the pain and suffering that he'd been subjected to over the course of his life.

If Marcus was to die here, he wanted to ensure that his pain lived on in a surrogate long after he was gone.

And who better to carry this burden than his mother? Than the woman who had failed to protect her son from abuse, who had neglected to give him love or support, or to provide him with basic human needs.

Or, maybe, just maybe, this was the *real* plan all along.

"No!" Drake screamed when he finally realized what the object in Marcus Slasinsky's hands actually was.

By the time Drake fired a shot of his own, three muzzle flashes had already erupted from the barrel of Marcus' handgun.

Chapter 66

Georgina Adams was thrust forward with every bullet that tore into her back. When the third round struck her spine, she twisted and collapsed into Chase's arms.

"Georgina!" Chase screamed. Her sister nearly toppled her, and it was all she could do to stop them both from falling. After regaining her balance, Chase wrapped her arms around Georgina and lowered her to the ground.

Chase was screaming incoherent words that melted together in a cacophony of grief. The idea that she might be the target of the shooter never even crossed her mind.

Howling, she realized that her sister was still alive, if barely, and her lips were moving ever so slightly. Chase leaned down only to pull back when Georgina coughed up blood that speckled her pale cheeks.

"Georgina, no, no, please," Chase begged.

But there was nothing to be done now. As soon as Georgina started to shake, Chase knew that it was all over.

It was too late.

She'd finally found her sister, but it was too late.

Chase's tears dripped down on Georgina's face and mixed with her blood, causing the dark red streams to become a rosy pink.

"I'm sorry," she sobbed. "I'm sorry, I'm sorry, I'm so sorry."

Georgina blinked once, twice, and then her eyes rolled back. Chase shook her sister until the woman's blue eyes rotated and focused on her.

This time, when her mouth moved, Chase realized that she could understand the words, thick as they were with blood.

"I remember," Georgina whispered.

Chase started to rock her sister's head in her lap.

"I remember, Chase," Georgina repeated, just above a whisper. "And I… and I…"

Chase was inconsolable now.

They were going to be separated once more, but this time, no amount of police work, determination, or resolve would bring them together again.

Georgina coughed and then fell still. Chase thought her sister was gone, but then she inhaled one final, deep breath.

"Chase, I forgive you. I remember, and I forgive you."

Chapter 67

THE BULLET FROM DRAKE'S gun tore into Marcus Slasinsky's side, sending him spiraling to the weed-covered ground. As he fell, his gun flew from his hand and buried itself in the overgrown flora.

Drake sprinted forward and found Marcus lying on his back, his arms outstretched. Moans of pain and shrieks of agony now filled the gardens, but they weren't coming from the serial killer. In fact, the man wasn't grimacing, wincing, or even frowning.

He was smiling.

Drake straddled Marcus and pointed his gun directly between the man's eyes.

"Took you long enough."

"Shut your mouth," Drake warned.

Marcus laughed.

"I could have hit her, Drake. I could have hit Chase. I could have killed Mommy."

"Shut your fucking mouth!"

Drake glanced over his shoulder and saw that while both Chase and Georgina were lying on the stage, it was the latter who was in a prone position.

"If I wanted to, I—"

Drake picked up his left foot then brought it down again on Marcus' side that leaked blood. While the man stopped speaking for a moment, his expression didn't change.

"The pain is gone, Drake. The pain is all gone. You should know that by now. Which is why I shot Georgina and not Chase."

As if responding to the mention of her name, Chase screamed.

Drake clenched his jaw and shook his head, trying to block out the sound.

"But now, now that Georgina is dead, my pain will live on. My pain will live on in Chase."

Drake squeezed his eyes closed, and yet tears somehow still managed to spill down his cheeks.

When he opened them again, the hand holding the gun was younger and the man on the ground wasn't Marcus Slasinsky but Dr. Mark Kruk. He was even sporting his round spectacles, and his hair was thick and full.

"You killed my partner," Drake hissed. "You killed my partner, you sick fuck."

"I'm not dead!" he heard Chase shout from behind him. Her voice had an airy, ethereal quality to it. "I'm not dead, Drake! I'm right here! I'm right here! *Please!*"

Drake blinked again and shook his head. When he turned his attention back to the man half-buried in foliage, it was Marcus Slasinsky again.

"You couldn't kill me back then, and you can't do it now," the man said, his smile growing ever wider.

Drake stared into the man's flat eyes. It was like a horrible recurring nightmare being back here with this animal, standing over him, his gun aimed at his face.

Somewhere, deep down, he knew that this nightmare would never end so long as Marcus was still among the living. It would take years, decades, maybe, but the man would either escape again or convince some sympathetic congressman that he was rehabilitated.

Then Marcus would be out, and this cycle of revenge would start all over again.

Chase bawled, and Drake turned to look at her. The woman was on her knees, her chin pointed to the sky, her mouth open.

He could barely make her out through the thick, green vegetation.

Vegetation that reminded him not of New York City, but the jungles of Columbia.

He turned back to Marcus.

"I'm not the same man I used to be," he said dully. The man's smile finally vanished. "And I think maybe there's a little more pain left in this world for you, Marcus."

Then he pulled the trigger.

Chapter 68

"CHASE, SHE'S GONE," A familiar voice informed her.

But Chase refused to look away from her sister's face, even though it had been some time since her eyes had gone blank and she'd stopped moving.

"Chase."

A hand came down on her shoulder, jarring her out of her stupor. She turned and looked up.

"I'm sorry," Drake said softly. His expression was soft, but his jaw was hard. He tried to help her up, but she remained rooted on the stage. She refused to do anything, knowing that if she let go of Georgina, then her sister really was gone.

I forgive you.

"Marcus?" the word came out of her mouth as a breathy whisper.

The muscles in Drake's jaw clenched even harder.

"He won't be bothering either of us anymore."

Chase knew that this news should be reassuring, that she should be happy that it was over, but she felt nothing.

She was hollow, empty.

Time passed; it could have been minutes, or hours, or days. Chase had no idea how long she sat there with Drake's hand on her shoulder, Georgina's head in her lap. Eventually, she heard a commotion and shouting voices that she recognized, but she still couldn't bring herself to let Georgina go.

Someone to her left coughed, drawing Chase's attention.

"Louisa?" she asked.

Louisa's eyes fluttered but didn't open.

"Louisa?"

This time someone replied, but it wasn't Louisa.

It was the voice of a young girl.

"Mommy? I found this butterfly. Isn't it… isn't it beautiful?"

Chase turned around and saw a young girl in a white dress moving through the weeds toward them. Her face was round and pink, and her eyes were a bright green.

Georgina.

"Come on, Chase—you need to get up. There are still people in this world who need you," Drake reminded her.

Even this failed to get Chase moving. But something else did.

It was the butterfly. Resting on the girl's pale knuckles was a single, orange Monarch butterfly. In the past, Chase would have been repulsed at the sight of such an insect, but not now.

Now, it was one of the most beautiful things that she'd ever seen. Tears streaming down her cheeks, Chase slowly lowered Georgina's head to the stage. As she did, the butterfly took flight, rising majestically toward the geodesic dome above. Chase followed the insect with her eyes and watched as it reached the pinnacle of the dome and then escaped into the night through a hole in the rotting plywood.

Drake was right.

Her sister might be gone, but there were still people who needed her.

And she refused to let them down.

Chapter 69

THE SCENE THAT FLOYD encountered inside the Butterfly Gardens was one of carnage. As soon as he burst through the doors, with Dunbar and two EMTs in tow, he caught the unmistakable whiff of death.

He found Marcus Slasinsky first. The man was lying in the grass with his arms and legs spread, blood pooled by his right side.

There was a single bullet hole in the center of his forehead.

Floyd didn't even give the man a second look as he continued toward the stage in the center of the dome. Drake, who was tending to Louisa, who was barely conscious, but very much alive, saw him approach and gave an approving nod.

Floyd found the second victim, Georgina Adams, with her arms crossed over her chest, next. Three distinct trails of blood led away from her body.

"Chase?" he gasped, his eyes darting.

Please be alive, Chase. Please.

His heart nearly broke when he spotted his partner.

Chase Adams was standing in the tall grass, tears glistening on her cheeks. She was gently nestling a young girl against her navel.

Floyd had never seen the girl before, but that didn't matter; he knew who she was. He could tell by the freckles spattering across the bridge of her nose, by her bright eyes, her brown hair that had a slight orange tinge to it.

Floyd walked up to her, put on his best smile, and crouched down low.

"Hi," he said, wiping tears from his face. "My name's Floyd, what's your name?"

The little girl looked at him, but instead of saying anything, she deferred to Chase first.

Chase sniffed and nodded, giving her permission to speak to this stranger.

The girl's green eyes returned to Floyd.

"My name's Georgina," she said. "It's nice to meet you."

Epilogue

FBI AGENT JEREMY STITTS turned his head toward his hospital room door. He'd had many visitors over the past week or so, but this was a first.

"What the hell?"

A black lab scrambled through the door, its long tongue lolling out of its mouth. The dog tried to jump up onto the bed, but one of its back legs was a little gimpy. Instead, it put its front two paws on the side of the cot and wagged its tail incessantly.

"Piper?"

The dog barked an affirmation, and a now smiling Stitts reached over and pulled the animal up onto the bed with him. Piper immediately started licking his face. She was so excited that her tail knocked the oxygen sensor from Stitts' finger, but he didn't care.

"Piper!"

The dog stopped licking him just long enough to bark again.

"I heard you were in need of a companion," a female voice said from the doorway. "And it looks like I didn't make the cut."

Stitts guided Piper's head out of the way to get a better look at who was speaking.

"Chase!" he exclaimed.

Chase grinned and stepped forward. She looked thin, but her face had some color to it.

"You look like shit," she stated.

"Auntie Chase! That's a bad word!" a high-pitched voice proclaimed.

Confused, Stitts leaned down even further. A cute girl who was maybe six or seven years of age, with green eyes and auburn hair, entered the room after Chase.

"Shit, you're right, Georgina. Another quarter for the swear jar, I guess," Chase said with a grin.

"And who's this?" Stitts asked, playing the game.

The little girl held Chase's hand tightly and nuzzled into her hip.

"Georgina," she said softly.

"Well, Georgina, you tell your auntie that if she swears again, it's not just going to be a quarter in the jar, but a hundred-dollar bill."

The girl's eyes went wide, and she looked up at Chase.

"A hundred? That's a lot!"

Chase laughed.

"Yeah, that's a lot. It seems like I've been giving out hundreds left, right, and center lately." Her face suddenly grew serious. "Listen, Georgina, can you go with Detective Dunbar for a moment? I need to talk to my friend Stitts."

The girl nodded and then started out of the room.

"It was nice to meet you, Georgina."

"It was nice to meet you too, Mr. Stitts."

Dunbar appeared in the doorway. He took the girl's hand and gave Stitts a nod.

Stitts returned the gesture.

When it was just the three of them—Stitts, Chase, and Piper—he let out a long sigh.

"I'm done, Chase. I'm done with the FBI, I'm done with all that. Can't take it anymore."

Stitts liked to pull the Band-Aid off quickly but was surprised by Chase's reaction.

Or lack thereof.

"I figured as much; that's why I got you a friend. Had to pull some strings, but Piper is retired, as you know."

Again, at the mention of her name, the dog barked. Stitts scratched her behind her ears.

"You gonna be okay?"

Chase shrugged.

"I'll be fine. You think that, what, because we slept together one time, that now I'm indebted to you for life? Are we imprinted on each other, now?"

Stitts' face went slack. But then Chase smiled, and he started to laugh. She joined him and they laughed for a good while.

"I love you, Stitts," Chase said after catching her breath.

"I love you too, Chase."

Then Stitts burst out laughing again.

***

"So far as I'm concerned, your sister was one of Marcus Slasinsky's victims, just like Stitts and Louisa," Director Hampton said.

Chase nodded.

"Thank you."

The man leaned back in his chair and pinched the bridge of his nose. Chase couldn't remember ever seeing him like this before: tired, emotionally exhausted, defeated.

In fact, up until recently, she never knew the man to have emotions at all.

"Stitts isn't coming back," Hampton said at last. "I gave him an extended leave in case he changes his mind."

"I know."

A silence fell over the two of them and Chase glanced around. The walls were decorated with service medals, various medals of honor, and two diplomas: one in criminal forensics and the other in criminal psychiatry.

What was missing was a photograph of the man's family.

If he had one.

Director Hampton leaned forward.

"Here's the thing, Chase: so far as the public is concerned, you're dead. You can thank your friend Drake for that, for sending the photograph to CNN. I don't have any desire to correct them, and I doubt you do, either. You can disappear, Chase. Take that little niece of yours and go live somewhere warm—anywhere but Florida. Go live a quiet life."

Chase stared at the man for a moment before rising to her feet.

"I'll think about it," she said, extending her hand.

Director Hampton extended his own.

When their fingers met, nothing happened. No spark of memories, of flashbacks, of subconscious narratives.

It was just a normal, traditional handshake between colleagues.

"If you do decide to move on, I just wanted to let you know that you're one hell of an agent and, on behalf of the entire Bureau, I want to thank you for your service. If ever you change your mind, we'll be more than happy to take you back, Chase."

***

"How'd that go?" Drake asked as he pushed himself away from the wall.

"Fine," Chase replied as she stepped out of the FBI Training Academy. "People treat me like a piece of precious glass, something that they need to handle with kid gloves so that I don't break."

Drake made a *hmph* sound as he fell into his stride beside her.

"What they don't realize, is that I'm already broken."

"That's what they make tape for," Drake remarked.

Chase stopped walking and surprised even herself by giving the man a big hug.

"And glue," she whispered in his ear as she let him go.

In the parking lot, Chase spotted Detective Dunbar standing in the open door of an unmarked car.

He wasn't waiting for her, Chase knew, but for Drake.

"Thanks for everything, Drake. I don't know how many people in this world I can count on, but I know I can count on you."

"I'm not sure—"

Chase leaned up and kissed the man on the cheek.

"For once, can't you just shut the fuck up?"

Drake looked at her, then a grin formed on his lips.

"I'm going to have to keep my mouth shut if I want to survive prison, so I figure I should run it as much as possible before Dunbar takes me back."

Chase raised her gaze to Dunbar, who had a stern expression on his face.

"Yeah, I'm not so sure that that's where you're headed. I have connections, you know."

The smile slid off Drake's face.

"I had connections, too—fuck, I knew the sergeant, Detective Dunbar, all the main players. A whole lotta good that did me."

Chase waited for a moment before answering.

"You know what your problem is?"

"You have an hour?"

Chase ignored the comment.

"Your problem is that all of your connections are on the inside. My connections? They have something that yours don't."

"And what might that be?"

"Money."

With that word still hanging in the air, Chase left Drake and started toward her car.

"You decide what you're going to do, Chase?" Drake hollered after her.

Chase didn't turn. She just continued to walk toward her BMW, her eyes locked on the young black man with short hair and a goofy grin on his face who was seated in the passenger seat.

"No, not yet. But could you imagine leaving Floyd without a partner? Because I sure can't."

END

Author's Note

I LOVE WRITING STORIES that weave together characters from different series'. *Painted Ladies* contains perhaps the most mixed cast of all my books, and while part of the focus was on undeniably on Damien Drake, it was still, in my mind, a quintessential *Chase* book. And yet, it deals with many common fears shared by my characters, with one notable exception (because Beckett's dead, baby). Marcus Slasinsky was the original protagonist in what I refer to as 'Drake's World', which contains Chase, Drake, Beckett, and Tommy Wilde, among others. He was the villain in Butterfly Kisses and he never left my mind since he was created on paper more than two years ago. I knew Marcus was going to come back and haunt Drake, but what I didn't know is the impact that he was going to have on Chase's life, as well. I wrote *Painted Ladies* to be enjoyed even if you haven't read any of Drake's books, but if you want to know more about his origins, then grab a copy of Butterfly Kisses. I mean, aside from Marcus, it's also the first introduction to Chase Adams... so what are you waiting for?

What's next for Chase, you ask? Is she really going to retire, or is she going to return with a new partner?

Spoiler alert: Book 8 in the Chase Adams Series, *Adverse Effects*, is already up on pre-order. Chase **will** return, but nothing about her life—or her world—will ever be the same.

And now it's that time—time for the obligatory request for a review. With four or five series' either starting up or on the go, I need to know which ones you guys want to continue reading. In an ideal world, I would have a dozen or so series set in

New York with characters weaving in and out of Drake's World, but the reality is, I need to prioritize writing *your* favorite characters. So, please, leave a review for *Painted Ladies* on Amazon to make sure that Chase can continue to hunt down evil in Drake's, or her, World.

As always,

You keep reading, and I'll keep writing.

Best,
Pat
Montreal, 2019

Made in the USA
Monee, IL
10 October 2020